3/14

THE
SLAYER
CHRONICLES

SECOND
CHANCE

▼

· HEATHER BREWER ·

THE SLAYER CHRONICLES

SECOND CHANCE

DIAL BOOKS

An imprint of Penguin Group (USA) Inc.

This is dedicated to my big sister, Dawn Vanniman,
who has always believed in me.
And to the many people who haven't.

▼   ▼   ▼

DIAL BOOKS • *An imprint of Penguin Group (USA) Inc.*

PUBLISHED BY THE PENGUIN GROUP

Penguin Group (USA) Inc., 375 Hudson Street, New York, NY 10014, U.S.A. • Penguin Group (Canada), 90 Eglinton Avenue East, Suite 700, Toronto, Ontario, Canada M4P 2Y3 (a division of Pearson Penguin Canada Inc.) • Penguin Books Ltd, 80 Strand, London WC2R 0RL, England • Penguin Ireland, 25 St. Stephen's Green, Dublin 2, Ireland (a division of Penguin Books Ltd) • Penguin Group (Australia), 250 Camberwell Road, Camberwell, Victoria 3124, Australia (a division of Pearson Australia Group Pty Ltd) • Penguin Books India Pvt Ltd, 11 Community Centre, Panchsheel Park, New Delhi—110 017, India • Penguin Group (NZ), 67 Apollo Drive, Rosedale, Auckland 0632, New Zealand (a division of Pearson New Zealand Ltd) • Penguin Books (South Africa) (Pty) Ltd, 24 Sturdee Avenue, Rosebank, Johannesburg 2196, South Africa • Penguin Books Ltd, Registered Offices: 80 Strand, London WC2R 0RL, England

Library of Congress Cataloging-in-Publication Data
Brewer, Heather.
Second chance / by Heather Brewer.
p. cm.—(The Slayer chronicles; 2)
Summary: Joss is summoned by Abraham to New York City and told he must prove his loyalty to the Slayer Society by successfully leading a team in hunting a murderous Manhattan vampire, or his life will be forfeit. • ISBN 978-0-8037-3760-0 (hardcover)
[1. Vampires—Fiction. 2. New York (N.Y.)—Fiction. 3. Horror stories.]
I. Title.   PZ7.B75695Sec 2012   [Fic]—dc23   2012001501

Designed by Jason Henry • Text set in Meridien • Printed in the U.S.A.
1 3 5 7 9 10 8 6 4 2

► ACKNOWLEDGMENTS ◄

Not many people can say that they have an incredible team of people behind them, supporting their goals of world domination. But I'm one of the lucky few, and I owe each of them an enormous amount of gratitude.

First, to my editor, Liz Waniewski, for being awesome and brilliant and everything that I want to be when I grow up (if I grow up, that is). You make me a better writer, Liz, and I hope you realize that Joss wouldn't be Joss without you. Second, to my fabulous agent, Michael Bourret, who has talked this overly dramatic author off the fictional ledge I can't say how many times, and who's offered so much good advice, encouraging words, and amazing friendship, I honestly don't know where I'd be without him.

Huge, squishy hugs to my penguins over at Penguin Young Readers. I'd name you all by name, but honestly, I know I'd forget someone. You're my family, penguins, and together we're reaching those world domination goals. Thank you!

And thanks, of course, to the Minion Horde. You keep reading. I keep writing. I love you all more than you will likely ever understand. There are worlds inside of us, Minions, and it's so cool to have someone to explore them together. (Even if some of those worlds are dark and scary.)

Paul, Jacob, and Alexandria . . . what can I say? You've seen me through eight books now, and more smiles, tears, laughter, fears, and ice teas than I can count. You are my everything, and every word that I write is for you.

CONTENTS

▼ ▼ ▼

THE
SLAYER
CHRONICLES

SECOND
CHANCE

▼

PROLOGUE

Kilian whipped around the corner of the building, his long hair flowing behind him, his coat billowing in the wind. His heart beat steadily in an unhurried pace. His breaths came even and smooth. But Kilian was terrified and didn't know where to go, or who could possibly help him. He was alone now but for his tormentors. His brother, Jasik, was nowhere to be found. Perhaps they'd killed him. Perhaps Kilian had no brother now. He pressed his back against the brick wall, sinking as deeply as he could into the shadows, hoping against all reason that the vampires who'd been hunting him would give up their chase.

His stomach rumbled, and inside Kilian's mouth, his fangs elongated. He was hungry. Famished. He hadn't had a drop of blood to eat for two days. He needed sustenance. Especially if he was going to be forced to face off with four vampires who were much older, much craftier, and much stronger than him. But the city streets were eerily quiet, and even though Kilian was straining his ears to listen, he couldn't hear any human heartbeats in the near vicinity.

But he did hear something. Something that made his breath catch in his throat, and his hands clench into nervous fists at his sides.

Laughter. And footsteps. He wasn't certain which scared him more. But he did know that both belonged to four different people. And those people, those vampires, were headed straight for him.

"Come out, come out, wherever you are," called a singsongy voice that he could only attribute to Boris. Kilian turned his head, peering down the street—at first in the direction that the voice had come from, and then the other way. There was no escaping them, that much he knew. He could run, but they would find him. They were relentless, and nothing he could do would stop their pursuit of him.

But that didn't mean he wasn't going to try.

With a deep breath, he darted down the street with vampiric speed. He came to a stop several alleys over.

His ears were greeted with only a moment's silence before the brothers found him once again. This time, it was Kaige who spoke. "You'd think a vampire would remember that a rush of adrenaline only makes the blood taste that much sweeter."

Laughter, cold and hollow, followed. Then a smaller, less-confident voice chimed in with marked hesitancy. "The Council's put a warrant out for us. Maybe it would be wise to stop killing humans in the open now, and beg for Em's forgiveness. She might be lenient."

"Lenient? When in Em's existence has she ever proven to be lenient when a vampire has broken the law?" Their voices put them just around the corner from Kilian. And even though there were a million places he could run, Kilian felt trapped. A thread of panic tickled its way up his spine.

"Curtis is right, Sven. Em will kill us for our crimes. That is, unless we give her reason not to." Kilian could hear the smirk on Boris's lips. "That little stunt pulled by Slayers in the Catskills last summer? I just got wind that the Slayer Society's calling that group in to deal with us. If we bring her the head of the Slayer responsible, she might find it in her stone-cold heart to forgive our crimes."

"What about our friend here?"

Kilian darted his eyes all around, but couldn't see them, couldn't even sense their presence anymore as the terror took hold of him at last. He couldn't breathe, could barely move, and the exhaustion of running from them was finally catching up to him.

"Taking the life of a fellow vampire would be breaking the highest law. Is handing over one Slayer really going to ease Em's temper after that?"

His fingers were trembling as he traced his hand along the brick wall, stepping back, deeper into the alley. He had to get away from them long enough to regroup his thoughts, to quell his panic. If he didn't regain control of himself . . .

"Over twenty died in that blast. I say we kill him."

"So do it already."

A hand reached out from the darkness.

Teeth followed.

· 1 ·

THE SAD REALITY

Joss lifted his suitcase from the trunk of his dad's car and turned to say something to his dad—something light and conversational about how it was good to be home, even though it wasn't, not really—but the side door of the gray house that they now called home was already slamming closed. So much for his homecoming. The drive from the airport had been long and silent—a strange, indescribable tension hanging in the air between he and his dad. It was like riding in the car with a stranger who couldn't stand the sight of you. Worse, though. Far worse. Because the stranger was his father.

The silence had given Joss time to reflect on the

school year that he'd just spent away, however. Not that they were pleasant memories. In the beginning they had been. Joss had lived with his favorite cousin, Henry, and had befriended a boy named Vlad. Only Vlad turned out not to be a boy at all, but instead a vampire.

Just like Sirus.

Joss had been duped twice now by vampires, taunting him with the gift of friendship, only to have them rip it away again with their horrible, menacing fangs. He was done with friends. He was done with searching for companionship. He only had his want of vengeance now, and the sense of duty and honor that had been given to him by the Slayer Society.

And his stake, of course.

Inside his right front jeans pocket, his cell phone buzzed to life. He withdrew it and flipped it open to read the incoming text message. It was her. Again.

He wasn't exactly certain how Kat had gotten his cell number. But she'd been sending him messages for days now—each one more troubling than the last.

This one was brief: ARE YOU GOING HOME FOR THE SUMMER, JOSS? MUST BE NICE TO HAVE A FAMILY TO GO HOME TO. I'M COMING FOR YOU. DON'T FORGET IT.—K

He chewed the inside of his cheek briefly, considering a reply. But then thought better of it and flipped the phone closed again.

Kat would have to wait.

He shut the trunk and lugged his bag across the lawn to the door, remembering a time when he and his family had lived in a yellow house. A house that had been filled with sunshine and laughter and love. It felt like those memories had transpired over a million years ago, in a time that they'd all forgotten. For a brief moment, Joss wondered if that time—when Cecile had been alive and their family had been whole—had just been a dream. But then he shook his head. No. It couldn't have been a dream. Not one of Joss's, anyway. His dreams were dark. His dreams were awful, haunting images that never let the goose bumps on his flesh settle. His dreams were nightmares. Nightmares about Cecile.

As he moved toward the house, he thought about the dreams that had been tormenting him since his sister's demise, about how they usually featured flowers in some way, and he wondered if they would ever stop. But he also wondered if they were just dreams, or if—as crazy as it sounded—Cecile was reaching out from beyond the grave, hell-bent on revenge. He didn't like having those thoughts—so much so that he usually pretended that he never had them—but the fact was that he spent too much time worrying about his dream sister in ways that he had never worried about Cecile. The dream Cecile scared him more than anything, even vampires, and he always felt so powerless against her. She carried messages with her, messages of his impending doom, impending death, and he worried, as silly as it seemed, that his death would not come from his job as a Slayer. But from Cecile herself.

It was stupid to think those things. And if ever asked, Joss would have laughed off the notion that he believed his dreams could ever physically hurt him. But the truth was, he wasn't at all convinced that they couldn't.

As he pulled open the screen door and lifted his bag over the threshold, he spied his mother sitting at the dining room table, that faraway look in her eye. Joss knew that look well, as it had been growing steadily worse every day since Cecile had died. His mother was a fragile creature, in ways that she had never been fragile before. He kept his voice low, so as not to startle her. "Hi, Mom. How are you?"

She glanced up from her sad fog and nodded, forcing a small smile. It made Joss's heart break to see his mother acting as well. "Fine, Joss. I'm just fine. How was your trip, dear?"

Stepping inside, he closed the door behind him and set his suitcase beside the laundry cabinet. "It was interesting. A lady sitting beside me on the plane was very chatty."

"Nice chatty?"

In a moment of pure awkwardness, he simply nodded and smiled. They were both actors now, and he hoped against hope that his mother couldn't see through his facade the way that he could see through hers.

He pulled a chair out and sat down at the table, grateful for this time, this moment with his mother before his father started in on him about something he'd done wrong in the five seconds he'd been home. Their relationship—his and his dad's—had changed dramatically since Cecile's funeral. His father had pulled away into a protective cocoon, and no amount of hugs or talks or high fives could break through that barrier. It was as if, through Cecile dying, his entire family had perished as well. He would have done anything to change it, to turn back time and have his family again. But there was nothing, Joss was slowly realizing, that he could do to restore their happiness. So he was doing the next best thing: hunting down the vampire that had destroyed them all. And when he found the beast, he was going to make it suffer.

"Joss." The look on his father's face as he entered the room was one of irritation. "Take care of your luggage. I shouldn't have to tell you that. You're old enough to start taking some real responsibility around here."

Joss's ears burned slightly. If his dad only knew that he was incredibly responsible, that he'd been charged with saving humankind, that he was someone that the world was unknowingly relying on for support. . . .

But his dad didn't know that, would never know that. As Abraham had taught Joss, being a Slayer was a thankless job, and one that had to be kept in the strictest secrecy. Even from your parents.

"Sorry, Dad. I'll take care of it right away." Joss pushed his chair back and stood, reaching immediately for his suitcase.

As his father turned from the room, he grumbled, "And we still have to discuss that report card of yours, young man."

Joss wrapped his fingers around the handle of his suitcase and picked it up, letting his eyes follow his father out of the room. He missed his dad more than anything—maybe even more than he missed Cecile—but he knew, deep down, that the father he had known and loved was gone for good, forever changed by an experience that haunted them all like a shadow in the corner of every room. With a heavy heart, he moved up the stairs to his bedroom without another word.

He'd only been to the room once before, just long enough to move some boxes inside. Then he was in the car and on his way to the airport, his dad lecturing him on how to behave while he was living at Aunt

Matilda and Uncle Mike's house. He hadn't even had a chance to unpack before moving on to Bathory, to a life that would bring him in close contact with a vampire called Vladimir Tod. He clenched his fists at the thought before entering his room.

His bed was unmade, and lining the walls were piles of small boxes, containing most of Joss's insect collection and books. The room looked more like a temporary storage facility than a teenage boy's bedroom, and didn't exactly provide the "welcome home" feeling he'd been daydreaming about. He lifted the bag and set it on top of the trunk at the foot of his bed, then retrieved a set of sheets, blanket, and pillow from the linen closet in the hall. For now, anyway, this house was home to him, so it was time to settle in and remind his parents in whatever subtle way that he could manage that they hadn't lost both of their children that night. They still had a son.

After making his bed, he reached for a box on top of the nearest stack and pulled it down, setting it on the floor by his feet. He crouched and tore the lid free from the packaging tape that had held it closed. Inside, under a wad of newspaper, were a stack of carefully bubble-wrapped frames. At a glance, he recognized them as some of his favorite collected specimens. He lifted them out and set them gently on the bed, then returned his attention to the box. The remainder of it was filled with books. Looking around the room briefly, Joss located his bookcase and picked up an armful of books. It was time to get to work. Time to put things away.

An hour later, his bed was crisply made, his bookcase was full and neatly organized, and the shelves on the wall were home to his favorite specimens. On his nightstand sat a small silver frame, containing a photograph of Cecile. Not nightmare Cecile, but real Cecile. The sweet, blond cherub who had brightened his life the moment he'd seen her in the hospital nursery.

He broke down the boxes as he emptied them, stacking the cardboard neatly in the hall outside his door. It was another mindless task—one where he didn't have to think about his shattered family or his botched private job or the betrayal of his closest non-family friend to date—and he welcomed it. He had seen too much in the past year of his life that he couldn't forget, that he couldn't numb away with the aid of video games and mass quantities of caffeine. And now, with the betrayal of Vlad, he was in danger of losing his cousin Henry as well. It was unbearable, to be so alone, to know that he had no one who he could rely on, that—apart from the Slayer Society—he was on his own. And the idea that Henry could even consider siding with a vampire against him! It sickened Joss. It hurt him. In ways that Henry could never understand.

So Joss needed mindless tasks. He needed a void in which he could tumble and roll without a care in the world, so far away from the harsh bleakness of his reality.

As he peeled the bubble wrap back from the framed Black Corsair, Joss smiled. This time it wasn't an act. This time it was a real, honest, actual smile, brought on by the love of his grandfather and the framed gift he'd bestowed upon Joss before he'd died. The Black Corsair was a large insect, and at first glance, there didn't seem to be anything vicious about it at all. But just try explaining that to the May beetle, the preferred victim of the assassin Corsair. The Corsair would attack from behind and hold on to their prey with the spongy pads on their legs. They were sneaky, these assassin bugs. Deadly. And no one would know it by looking at them. Just like a Slayer.

He'd wished he'd known that his grandfather had been a Slayer, but it was probably for the best that he hadn't. It was important for a Slayer to keep his position secret, especially from his family. Having that secret revealed could endanger them, and that was inexcusable. Family was important. More important, maybe, than anything else in the world.

His smile slipped, fading away just as quickly as it had come, and Joss set his prized possession on the bed. Stepping over the pile of cardboard, he moved back down the stairs and rummaged in the junk drawer for a hammer and nail. The Black Corsair, as in every house they'd lived in since he was eight, would hang in its place of honor over his bed.

Digging through the drawer, Joss frowned. In this house, much like every house they'd lived in, the nails and screws and batteries and tools and flashlights and weird things that had no place found their home in the junk drawer. But not a single nail was in the drawer. Furrowing his brow, Joss said, "Hey, Mom, where's a nail? I want to hang up my Black Corsair."

His mother was still sitting at the table, but now a steaming cup of tea sat on the table in front of her. Her fingers curled around it, as if huddling for warmth. The tea-bag string dangled over the cup's edge. He was about to ask her again, when something in her eyes shifted, as if the fog had momentarily lifted. "There's a box of them in the garage. Your father can show you."

He hesitated before he moved, mostly because he knew what would happen if he asked his father for a nail. They'd discuss his grades, or the fact that Joss needed a haircut, or something else that had nothing to do with the fact that his dad was still grieving and had turned Joss into the Invisible Boy. He bit the inside of his cheek until he couldn't bear it anymore. Then, on his way back upstairs, said, "It's okay. It can wait until later."

"Oh. Joss? I forgot. This came for you earlier."

When he turned back, his mother was sliding a large white envelope across the table toward him. Joss moved back down the steps, retrieved it, and headed upstairs. He was in his bedroom before he ripped the end of the envelope open. When the small parchment bundle tumbled out, his heart picked up its pace some. It was wrapped in a burgundy ribbon, and held closed with a wax seal that bore the initials S.S., meaning that it could only be from the Slayer Society. He wagered they were simply requesting his final notes on the reconnaissance he'd convinced them he'd done in Bathory, but hoped it was his new assignment, and that it would take him far away from this house and the emotional ghosts that haunted it.

Joss,

Your presence is required in Manhattan in two days time. There is private business to attend to. Bring your supplies and pack enough clothing for the entire summer. All arrangements have been made.

—Abraham

Downstairs, the phone rang shrilly, its metallic jingle echoing through the entire house. Joss heard his mother's voice, but not her words. Then moments later he heard his father's deep tones. Opening his suitcase, he emptied it of clean and dirty clothes and began repacking. If Abraham said he was going, he was going. And soon.

"Joss. Downstairs. Now."

His father's voice shook him to the core. What once had been immense and immeasurable sadness was now manifesting in his dad in strange, angry ways, and Joss wasn't sure which he preferred (though he honestly preferred neither). But he knew that whenever his father barked that he should immediately drop whatever he was doing and hurry to wherever his father was barking from, or he'd have hell to pay. So he jumped lightly over his cardboard pile, noting that he should pick it up before his dad saw the mess, and hurried down the stairs, where his parents were now both sitting at the kitchen table. Mom's mug of tea was half gone, its wrinkled tea bag lying on a spoon to its left. Joss stood at the end of the table somewhat awkwardly. "Yeah, Dad?"

"Your uncle Abraham just called." The look in his father's eyes said that this was something that shouldn't surprise Joss, like he'd orchestrated whatever excuse Abraham had given for getting Joss to Manhattan for the summer. But Joss stood stone-faced, revealing nothing that might so much as hint at the fact that he was privy to more information than his suspicious father. After a moment, his father spoke again. "He's working in conjunction with the Natural History Museum in New York this summer, and thought it might be a good experience for you to tag along, act as an intern. He thought that perhaps the discipline of a job might spark some semblance of responsibility in you. And your mother and I agree."

Relief flooded through Joss—relief that he hated to feel. Those feelings made him a bad person, a bad son—didn't they? He was thrilled to be going somewhere, anywhere, out of this house, away from the stress of being there, away from the pain of his day-to-day life. Anywhere was better than the shadow of his parents' grief. Besides, he was looking forward to seeing his fellow Slayers again. The summer before this one felt like it had happened a million years ago. He missed them. He even missed Abraham, and wondered if it was possible that Abraham had missed him—in ways that his own parents, apparently, had not.

"You get on a plane in two days, so you'd better get packed." Joss nodded and turned around, ready to walk back up the stairs. But he was given pause by his father's next words. "But pick up the damn boxes and stick them in recycling first."

His feet felt lighter with the aid of his newfound relief as he moved back up the stairs, and the first thing that Joss did, without complaint, was to gather the pile of broken-down boxes into a heap in his arms and carry them downstairs and out into the garage. While he was out there, he retrieved the hammer and a single nail.

Once back in his room, he tapped the nail into the wall above his bed and carefully hung the Black Corsair in its place. He hoped that wherever his grandfather was in the ether, wherever he was on his Next Great Adventure, that he was looking on his grandson with an approving smile. Because Joss might not be the greatest student, the greatest cousin, the greatest friend, or even the greatest son . . . but he was a Slayer, like his grandfather before him. He was dedicated to a cause full of nobility and purpose. He was driven. He was bent on revenge for his withered home life. And though the reward would never be anything concrete, Joss knew that he was doing good. For mankind. For Cecile. For his grandfather.

And maybe, just a little, for himself.

• 2 •

HOMECOMING

Sunshine filtered through the branches of a large oak tree that loomed overhead like a watchtower. At first glance, Joss had no idea where he was. But he knew that tree. Knew it very well. Though he couldn't quite put his thumb on exactly where he knew it from.

The trunk was wider than he could wrap his arms around. Its crooked branches reached so high up into the sky that gazing up at them made Joss's head swim. But it might have been just any old oak tree, if it weren't for the striking feeling of familiarity that clutched Joss tightly in its grasp.

An image flashed in his mind. It was bright and quick, but so real that he sucked in a breath before grinning and running around the massive trunk to the other side. The image was a memory—one that came from the day his cousin Henry had first come to visit them at their new yellow house. As he whipped around the tree, the memory engulfed him, and all he could do was smile.

Henry couldn't have been more than eight years old at the time, but it was already clear which of the two of them was in charge of their friendship. Henry made the decisions, and Joss dealt with the aftermath—which usually ended with them in trouble, but was always a spectacular amount of fun. Henry didn't worry about taking care of his sibling, or being a good example. That was his brother, Greg's, job. Henry was the youngest. Like Cecile was in Joss's family. And that meant freedom.

They'd come to the tree so that Henry could show Joss something he'd brought with him that summer. And though Joss's heart was racing at just what that something might be, and whether or not it would land them both in unimaginable amounts of trouble, he was also anxious to see what his cousin had hidden in the cup of his hand.

Henry looked around, to make certain they were alone, before holding his hand out and peeling his fingers back. In his palm lay a small pocketknife. Joss gawked at it a moment before speaking. "Wow. That's so cool! Where'd you get it?"

Henry beamed. "It's Greg's, but he won't care."

Joss watched as his cousin pulled the blade free, revealing the sheen of metal that had been hidden inside the ivory handle. He'd always envied Henry for having a brother. Not that Cecile wasn't perfectly nice, but the most she could possibly lend him was a baby doll. And, to an eight-year-old boy, a pocketknife would have been way cooler at the time. He sighed, his eyes on the blade, and said, "I wish I had a brother."

Henry was quiet for a moment, then his eyes brightened. "I'll be your brother, Joss."

A small lump formed in Joss's throat then. "Really?"

Henry nodded. "Really really. Watch this."

Henry stabbed the tip of the knife into the tree and dragged it down, cutting through the bark and into the wood beneath. Then he pulled it free and did it again, forming a crooked X on the trunk. When he was done, he wiped the blade clean on his jeans and closed the knife, slipped it into his pocket, and turned to look at Joss. "That X marks the spot where we became brothers, Joss. And as long as it's here, we'll always be brothers."

Joss's chest felt so heavy and full of love for his

cousin that he didn't really know what to say. After a long pause, searching for the right words, what he came up with was, "Forever, Henry?"

Henry grinned. "Forever and ever."

As the memory came to a close, Joss reached the other side of the tree. He traced his fingertips along the sunbaked *X* carving and allowed the smile to slip from his face with the realization that he was standing in the front yard of his old yellow house. The home his family shared when Cecile was still with them.

Slowly, he turned around, toward the house. Staring in disbelief at his surroundings, he crossed the grass, his sneakers sinking slightly into the lawn, and made his way around the side of the house. How could he be here? How was this even possible? Was he in the past? Had he been transported here somehow?

He turned the corner then, and his heart froze before picking up its pace slightly. Cecile was on her knees in the flower bed that edged the house, facing away from him, focused on her task. Ever so carefully, she picked up a small flowering plant and placed it in a hole she'd dug, before covering its roots with rich, black soil. As she moved through her task, she hummed a happy tune—one that reminded him of his mother. It was an endearing scene, watching his little sister plant flowers in the garden, so Joss had no idea why witnessing it set his nerves on edge. Apart from the fact that he knew the only way he could see Cecile was to travel back in time.

Without turning toward him, Cecile stretched her arm out, pointing to the spade that was lying just out of reach in the grass to her left. "Will you hand me the shovel, Jossie?"

After a moment of hesitation—one where he questioned whether or not he really had managed to travel back in time without realizing it, and why his sister was outside planting flowers unsupervised—Joss crept forward and crouched, plucking the spade from its spot in the grass, and held it out for her. "What are you planting, Cecile?"

She didn't respond with words, but instead began digging furiously with her hands, as if her task couldn't wait any longer for the spade that Joss was trying to give to her. Curiosity overtaking him, Joss leaned forward, peering over his sister's shoulder. The earth had been disturbed in a rather haphazard, desperate way, and several new flowers had been planted in crooked rows along the flower bed. And there, in the middle, poking up from the ground, gray and horrible, was a human pinkie finger.

Joss's heart raced, and his head began to spin. Why was Cecile digging in a place where a body was buried? Did she know about the corpse? Had she seen it? Who did that pinkie belong to, and why had the flower bed become their grave? Nausea pushed its way up Joss's intestines, his stomach, his chest, tickling the back of his throat. A dead body. A dead person. In the garden. But why?

His throat felt raw as he forced the next question out. "What are you doing, Cecile?"

Suddenly Cecile's hand closed over his wrist. He dropped the spade into the grass, his eyes growing ever wider at the image of Cecile's fingernails. They were long and sharp, almost clawlike, and Joss could feel them digging into his skin. He looked at Cecile, who at last turned her head toward him slowly. Her eyes were closed, and she was smiling. And when she spoke, her singsong voice sent a terrified chill through him. "I'm digging your grave, Jossie."

Joss pulled his hand back, but Cecile's grip tightened. In a moment of sheer panic, he yanked his hand free, her claws digging bloody tunnels through his skin. As he scrambled backward in a crab walk, his voice shook. The sun was gone now, no more warmth on his skin. There was only gray and cold and Cecile crawling slowly after him. "I'm not dead! I'm not dead, Cecile! That isn't me in the garden there."

His back met with the trunk of the oak tree—he had no idea he'd made it so far—and all he could do was stare at his sister as she crawled toward him with her eyes closed. "Oh, but you will be. You'll die at the hands of a monster, Jossie. The same way you let me die."

He swore that she could see him, even though she wasn't looking, not even a peek. Her clawlike nails dug into the earth. It was like she was pulling herself along the ground, making her way toward him. He stifled a scream. This was his sister. He had nothing to be afraid of. Did he?

Her left hand met his ankle and he jumped. Her skin was cold, too cold, and felt lifeless. Her claws dug into him and she climbed her way up his leg, her smile spreading as she moved. Her teeth were dark gray, with spots of black. The sight of them made Joss quiver, but he couldn't look away. "I'm dead, Jossie, and all because of you. And soon you'll be dead, too."

She moved until her face was mere inches from his—the smell of her breath was nauseating, like rotten meat. When Joss opened his mouth to speak, his throat went dry, and his voice came out in a harsh whisper. "But why, Cecile? Why will I be dead?"

Slowly, she reached up with one of her claw hands and petted Joss's cheek, leaving traces of dirt and Joss's blood behind. She tilted her head sweetly, as if some-where inside of this creature, his young sister still existed. "Because, Jossie. Because bad boys go to hell. Especially when they send their sisters there."

Tears welled in Joss's eyes. He opened his mouth

again, this time to say that he was sorry for everything that he hadn't done to rescue her the night she'd died, and for failing to avenge her death now that she was gone. But he didn't have a chance to speak.

Cecile opened her eyes, revealing deep, dark caverns of black that went on forever. She lunged forward then and Joss screamed—but not before he noticed two long fangs inside of her hungry mouth.

· 3 ·

BITTERSWEET REUNION

Joss sat up from his nightmare with beads of sweat clinging to his forehead. He was thankful, at that moment, to be almost the last person still on the plane—mostly because he wasn't certain he could handle the sidelong glances from strangers as he lost his cool. The nightmares were getting worse.

After powering on his phone again, and ignoring another text from Kat (I'VE DECIDED NOT TO HARM YOUR FAMILY IN ANY WAY. JUST YOU, JOSS. I'LL DO YOU THAT KINDNESS, THE WAY YOU DIDN'T FOR ME.—K), Joss stood and stretched. He retrieved his backpack from the compartment over his seat and navigated his way down the aisle, pushing away all thoughts of Kat and her threats. She couldn't touch him. Could she? In the end, wouldn't the Society offer him some protection? He was one of them, after all. But then . . . maybe they expected him to be strong enough to stand up to an untrained girl. At least, he thought she was untrained. But who knew what her father, Sirus, had taught her and not told him about? Sirus was, after all, immensely talented at keeping secrets. Like the fact that he was a vampire.

Joss forced a smile at the pretty blond flight attendant, and once she'd wished him a good day, he found his way up the ramp and into LaGuardia Airport. As Joss exited the security area, he breathed a sigh of relief. He'd been on too many flights this week, but thankfully, he sat alone this time, free of any obligation to smile politely as he partook in conversation he really didn't care about. He moved down the hall with purpose, his eyes sweeping the area around him, as always, for any sign of anyone who might not be a hundred percent on the human side. Everyone looked fairly normal as he walked, so he proceeded to the baggage claim area and waited at carousel number five for any sign of his black and purple suitcase, with the neon green luggage tag that read STEAL MY LUGGAGE, WASH MY CLOTHES.

Something hard pressed into Joss's back, and his

mind screamed "GUN!" His heart ceased its beats for a moment, in question of who exactly was behind him and why exactly they were threatening to assault him. A vampire wouldn't use a gun, so clearly the person was human. And what human would brandish a gun in an airport? He doubted that many would, given the security measures of the day. Turning his head slightly to the left, Joss glimpsed his assailant and rolled his eyes. "What are you doing, Ash?"

"Blowing you into forty-seven-million bits." Ash grinned. "Also, entertaining myself while we wait for your luggage."

Joss turned around then, knowing that Ash would never really cause him physical harm, and looked down at the Sharpie marker that Ash had been jabbing in his back. He raised an eyebrow, as if to ask Ash if that were really necessary, and Ash chuckled and grabbed him into a rough hug. "Good to see you, kid. But I barely recognized you. You must've grown a foot since last summer. You could pass for twenty, at least, if someone wasn't looking too closely. Everybody else is waiting for us back at our temporary base of operation. Let's find that bag of yours so the party can begin."

Joss gave Ash's back a pat as they hugged, and when they separated, a kind of peace settled over him. He was home, in a weird way. He'd finally received the warm welcome that he'd very much wanted from his mom and dad. The Slayers, after all, were family to him, and a family like no other. They knew all of Joss's secrets, all of his strengths and weaknesses.

Well, not *all* of his secrets. They knew nothing about the private job he'd taken hunting the Pravus vampire in Bathory. They also didn't know that he'd failed miserably to kill said vampire. Or that he'd become good friends with Vlad, the same way he'd become good friends with Sirus.

He was pretty sure they didn't know, anyway.

Once they'd located his suitcase and grabbed a cab to take them deep into the heart of Manhattan, Joss allowed himself a small moment of happiness. Last summer had been all about training to become a Slayer. This summer, he was a Slayer, ready to take on vampirekind and kick their undead butts into eternity. Thinking about his stake, Joss cast a glance at their cabbie, who was busy chatting in another language into his Bluetooth headset, and said, "Hey, Ash. How do you travel with your stake? I mean, you can't take it in your carry-on, right?"

Ash shook his head. "Nah. Gotta check it. Which sucks, considering how many vampires work in the airline industry. But you'll find out all about that once you earn your stake."

Joss paused. Dorian had delivered his great-great-

great-grandfather's vampire killing kit, complete with stake, to him at the end of last summer. He'd assumed it had been given to him at the instruction of the Society, but now he was wondering if that were the case. He didn't say anything to Ash, because the last thing he wanted to do was to have his only means of protection take away from him. So he and Ash chatted all the way to Greenwich Village about school, what it was like to live with his cousin Henry, and how it felt being solo for the first time. By the time the cab came to a halt in front of the brownstone that was to act as their base of operations, Joss was really looking forward to seeing the other members of their little group. After Ash paid the cabbie, they exited the cab, Ash collected his bag from the trunk, and they headed up the steps to the double front doors. Joss opened the door and stepped inside, holding it for his escort. From inside came Morgan's voice. "Ash? You back already?"

Something about the question didn't sit right with Joss. Mostly because it was a question. The Slayers knew exactly who was walking into their domain, no matter what time of day or night it was. So why the question? He looked at Ash, who also seemed a bit on edge. Ash reached into his inside jacket pocket and gripped his stake, placing a finger over his lips before he replied. "Yeah. Traffic was surprisingly light. Everything okay here?"

Joss's eyes locked on his suitcase, where his vampire slaying kit was locked safely away. He wondered if it was possible to get his tools out without alerting anyone they didn't want to alert, but he highly doubted it. So he stepped ever so carefully closer to Ash and followed his lead. Ash moved down the small hallway, pausing for a moment to gesture that Joss should take point. Joss wanted to argue. Take point? He didn't even have a weapon! But Ash was the Slayer with seniority here, so Joss stepped in front of him without question and readied himself for anything he could drum up in his dark imagination.

Morgan called out again, his voice full of suspicion. "We're in the parlor. You coming in?"

When Ash spoke again, his words were but a whisper. "Be right there."

Joss's heart was racing. He had no idea what they were walking into, and very much wished that he had his stake in hand. His eyes combed the hall for potential weapons. He was eyeing the legs of a small plant stand, one of which might make a suitable pseudostake in a pinch, but before he could decide whether or not that would be the best choice, Ash shoved him from behind, sending him stumbling into the parlor. Joss spun as he tripped over his own feet, trying desperately to recover, certain that vampires had somehow infiltrated their group. They were going to leap on him any second, and Joss was going to die. Or worse, be turned. He could think of no greater nightmare than that— not even the last nightmare he'd had about Cecile.

A strong arm grabbed him around the neck then, and Joss stomped hard on the assailant's foot with his heel. Cratian swore loudly, and released him, but Joss was free for only seconds until Paty swept his leg, knocking him on his back. As she looked down at him, she pointed a long finger to his face and said, with a sternness that made Joss want to behave, "Stop it. We were just playing with you. You're not being attacked."

It was only at that moment, ironically, that Joss felt the weight of her foot pressing into his chest, pinning him in place. He flicked his gaze around the room, finding Ash and Morgan in the corner stifling their laughter, and Cratian sulking a bit as he rubbed the soreness from his stomped toe. On a small table sat a white cake, with big red frosting flowers all along its top edge. Paty removed her foot and took his hand, helping him to his feet. Joss turned, confused, and looked around the parlor. Bookcases and an intricate fireplace lined the walls, and the only furniture in the room were two large, leather easy chairs and the table on which the cake sat. Words that formed a lump in his throat swirled across the top of the cake in black frosting: WELCOME BACK, JOSS!

They hadn't been overrun by vampires at all. His fellow Slayers were just trying to surprise him. Joss turned back to them, his heart so full of gratitude that it nearly burst, and managed to say, "Thank you."

Ash clapped his hands together. "Enough screwing around. Let's eat!"

Paty cut several slivers of cake and placed them on small paper plates, saving the biggest piece for Joss. They stood around, eating sugary yumminess and chatting, Joss's tension and sadness and looming sense of failure leaving him for the moment. As he swallowed a lump of red frosting, he said, "Where's my uncle, anyway?"

Cratian shrugged. "Abraham left pretty abruptly two days ago to fly to Headquarters in London. He gave us instructions to secure a temporary base of operations here and said to await his return for further orders. At this point, kid, you know about as much as we do about why we're all here."

The front door opened and a second later, slammed closed. Everyone in the room tensed, but no one spoke. Heavy footfalls carried Abraham, as if on cue, into the parlor. His face was drawn, as if something were troubling him. Joss tried to catch his eye, but before he could utter a word, his uncle said, "A man is dead."

Joss exchanged looks with his fellow Slayers, his

heart sinking fast. Who was dead? And why did knowing that sit in the pit of Joss's stomach like a hot coal? He turned back to his uncle, ready for anything.

He hoped, anyway.

▸ 4 ◂

ANYTHING

Joss followed behind his uncle, crossing yet another street, and turned down an alley. They'd left the brownstone immediately after Abraham's announcement, and Joss hadn't questioned it. After all, he was there to follow orders.

At the end of the alley stood a group of people. Three men, three women. Two of the men were looking back over their shoulders at the approaching Slayers. The rest were focusing on whatever was lying on the ground at the center of their group. As Joss approached with his team, he, Morgan, Paty, Ash, and Cratian exchanged looks. What was going on exactly?

Who was dead? Who were these people? Why were they here? And what exactly was causing the worried tingle that was crossing Joss's nerves?

This had nothing to do with Vlad, or with the fact that Joss had tried and failed to kill the creature, under a private contract. Did it?

No. That would be ridiculous. Joss was just panicking. As long as he managed to keep his cool, everything would be fine and Uncle Abraham would be none the wiser.

With a deep, calming breath, Joss followed the others deeper into the alley. His stomach roiled when he saw the body lying on the ground. Its neck had been torn open on one side, but curiously, there was no pool of blood on the pavement beneath it. For a moment, Joss's world tilted. But then it righted itself again. He'd never seen gore like this. Sure, he'd seen death before. But this seemed so deliberate, so . . . cruel.

A tall man with broad shoulders and stringy blond hair pressed a button on his cell phone and put it to his ear. "This is Mason. I need a cleanup in the alley between Tenth and Eleventh, off University Place. It's open to the street, so entry should be easy. A man's been killed. Fairly certain he was a victim of a vampire crime."

After a pause, he said, "No assisted exit needed. My team's on the scene."

He hung up, and as he slipped the phone into his pocket, he addressed Joss's Slayer family. "None of what I'm about to tell you leaves this group. Understood?"

Nods moved across the alley like a stadium crowd doing the wave. When they were finished, the newcomer continued. "We're the Slayer team responsible for protecting Manhattan. It's a daunting task, as the vampires seem to run wild here in the city. But lately, things have taken a turn for the worse."

His eyes fell to the fresh corpse. Joss's followed, but only for a moment, as he could feel his world tilting once again.

"There's a serial killer on the loose, and we're pretty damn sure it's a vampire. The victims have had their necks torn open, and are, in most cases, completely drained of blood. Local police think it's some kind of freak with a blood fetish, but this has vamp written all over it. The trouble is . . . we haven't been able to locate the killer."

With a glimmer of shame in his eyes, the man flicked a glance in Abraham's direction before continuing. "After meeting with the Society elders, it's been determined that perhaps our only option is to bring in a special-ops team to take the case over. And thanks to the skill demonstrated by young Mister McMillan here last summer in the Catskills, you're that team."

A small lump formed in Joss's throat, but he swallowed it quickly, despite his growing nausea. No one knew that the explosion he'd caused last summer that had killed Sirus and the other vampires had been an accident. Not for certain, anyway. But Joss had a feeling that his uncle Abraham was highly suspicious by the way he'd acted toward Joss after the explosion.

Joss couldn't tell his uncle the truth, that he hadn't really killed all of those vampires on purpose. Because that would make Joss both a liar and a coward. And he very, very much preferred to be viewed as a Slayer, rather than either of those things.

Besides, who was it hurting to keep that little detail to himself? No one. But if the truth got out . . . that's when the real pain would begin. The Society wouldn't be very forgiving that he'd deceived them, and he could only imagine how his Slayer team would react. Not to mention Uncle Abraham. No. This was a secret best kept tucked carefully in the back of Joss's mind, never to be spoken aloud.

"As far as this debriefing goes, I'm afraid we don't have much to report. There's no obvious pattern as to how the killer is choosing its victims. The victims themselves are pretty randomly chosen. Some men, some women. Ages ranging from the teen years to the elderly. Like I said, I'm afraid we don't know much. But then, I guess that's why the Society called you here." Mason pursed his mouth a bit, as if something bitter had settled onto his tongue. "What we can tell you is that all of the deaths that we believe are connected have taken place here in Manhattan. Largely in Midtown, but they've been spread out all over Manhattan. Plus, we've seen an increase in vamp activity in the last few weeks. It's like they're gathering for some kind of meeting or something. So . . . that's it. The show's all yours. We've been told to focus on the outer boroughs. Until this serial killer is taken care of, Manhattan belongs to you."

As if on cue, the other Slayers wordlessly filed back out the alley, eyeballing Abraham's team as they exited. It was clear to Joss that they weren't happy about handing over the reins, but what did they expect? If they had been charged with finding a killer and eradicating it, and had failed to do so, it was time for someone else to give it a go.

Morgan shook his head. "Am I getting this right? Is your team stepping completely aside?"

Mason pursed his lips a bit before answering. He was clearly unhappy with the change of pace, especially on his turf, but was stuck between a rock and a hard place. "On direct order of the Society . . . yes."

Paty stepped forward, shaking her head as well. "You can't step down without naming a new case handler. You know that. There are no assumptions in the Society."

Barely a heartbeat had passed before Mason's eyes fell on Joss. "Joss. You're calling the shots on this case."

Joss blinked. "What?"

"Believe me. It wasn't my decision to make this time, or I would have chosen Abraham."

Insult filled Joss to the brim. Just because he was only a teenager, Mason didn't think he was up to the task? That was bull crap. Joss met his eyes with a falsely confident raised eyebrow. False, because he had no real idea if he meant what he was about to say. But he wasn't about to let this guy know that. "I can do it. I can lead a team. I just . . . haven't yet."

A smirk appeared on Mason's face. "Well, I look forward to seeing you succeed. Everyone in the Society shares my sentiment, I'm sure."

Joss folded his arms in front of his chest. "Do you have any other pertinent information about the victims or killer, or are you just taking up space now?"

As Mason exited, he gave Joss's shoulder a firm squeeze, the look in his dark eyes full of meaning. "Good luck, little man."

Joss shook his shoulder away. He didn't need luck. He had skill and cunning.

The Slayers exited, and the rest of his team breathed

a collective sigh of relief. Something told Joss that Slayer teams tended not to intermingle, and maybe there was a good reason for that.

Paty was looking down at the dead man, her head tilted slightly to the side. "It's so sad. I wonder who he was. If he has a family."

A hand fell on Joss's shoulder, and he looked over to see Morgan, who pulled slightly, urging Joss to come with him. "Come on, kid. There's nothing to see here. Besides, Slayer teams aren't allowed to remain during cleanup."

"Why not?" It made sense to stay, to examine the scene, to assist in any cleanup that had to take place. So why were they leaving? Why was this something left to a mysterious Society crew, and not to the Slayers themselves?

Morgan leaned closer and spoke softly. "There are levels to the Society that you don't understand yet— hell, I'm not even sure I understand them all myself. But we were told early on to exit prior to cleanup, and we do as we're told. You'd be better off listening, kid. And not questioning the rules. Just trust me on this."

Joss did trust him. But he wasn't at all certain that he completely trusted the mysterious ways of the Slayer Society. Not that he dared put voice to his doubts. He trusted their beliefs, their actions, their wisdom, but their routines seemed just a little bit . . . off. Maybe it was because he was still green. Maybe he just needed time. That had to be it. They were the Slayer Society, after all. And he . . . he was just Joss.

"There's one more thing," Abraham spoke, his voice echoing slightly in the alley, even though his tone was eerily calm and even. Joss's heart beat solidly inside his chest. "The elders in London called me there to give me some rather disturbing news that I thought you all might find interesting. It seems my nephew took a private job in Bathory."

Joss widened his eyes and turned back to face his uncle. Morgan pulled his hand away and stepped back, as if Joss had spontaneously erupted in flames. Paty's fingers found her mouth, more horrified at the notion of Joss's betrayal than the murder victim lying before her. Ash and Cratian simply stared at him. A heavy air of disappointment filled the space. And Joss felt like he was shrinking, sinking down into the pavement, into the earth below.

If he could have, he would have.

Cratian shook his head. Shadows hung over the group. They looked like they'd been betrayed by one of their own. Largely because they had.

Joss looked from one Slayer to the next, avoiding

his uncle's eyes. He had no idea what to say. He'd been caught, and could offer up no explanation or apology that would right the wrong he had done. But all he could think of to say was, "I . . . I'm sorry. I just wanted to help my . . . my mother."

It wasn't a lie. His mother had been on every pill imaginable and attended therapy with many doctors since Cecile died. The bills were ridiculously high, adding stress to an already stressful time. And deep down, Joss wondered if maybe his father blamed his inaction that night for his mother's now-fragile mind. He was right to place that blame. Joss had tapped over that first domino in this scenario. As far as he was concerned, he was the one who'd stolen his family from himself. And he had no idea how to set it right again.

Abraham lowered his voice even further. Not so much that his words were a whisper, but so that Joss did have to focus on what he was saying in order to really hear him. "Joss has betrayed us, betrayed the Slayer Society. And by Society law, such a betrayal warrants the punishment of death."

The last spoken word echoed in Joss's mind, reverberating through every cell in his body. He was going to die. His Slayer family was going to kill him. Just moments ago, they were all eating cake and laughing.

Now he was going to perish in an alley at their hands for betraying them.

Paty chimed in then, her words full of sharp edges. "How could you, Joss? You know what we have to do now. You've given us no choice."

Abraham held up a hand, silencing her. His eyes were on Joss, whose life was flashing through his mind like an old 8mm film. "After much pleading on my part, and promises that I only hope I can fulfill one day, Headquarters has done the unthinkable. They've instructed me *not* to kill Joss."

Joss's heart beat twice, then paused for a moment before continuing its hesitant rhythm.

"Not yet, anyway. Not unless he fails in his new assignment." Abraham glared at him, utter disappointment oozing from his pores. "And let's make no mistake about this. This is your last chance to prove your loyalty to the Society. If you fail, or if you screw up even the tiniest bit in the future, we will kill you, Joss. It's what we do, and we're damn good at it. I put my neck on the line, vouching for you, begging the council to give you a second chance. If you mess this up, it won't just be bad for you. It'll be bad for me, for the team. Screwing this up would mean betraying us all in ways that cannot be forgiven. And we don't take betrayal lightly."

The harsh reality of his circumstances settled onto his nerves like clinging cobwebs. But there was no turning back now. He'd made his choice. He'd have to live with the consequences.

"Thank you." Joss blinked around at his fellow Slayers, guilt eating him alive. "Thank you for another chance. I . . . I'm so sorry. I won't—"

"Joss. Zip it." Ash's eyebrows had drawn together in anger. "Just listen to what your uncle has to say."

Immediately, Joss snapped his mouth closed and turned his attention to Abraham, who was now addressing the entire group, even though they all understood that this was Joss's task, and his alone. "Headquarters has charged Joss with hunting down and extinguishing the vampire responsible for the Manhattan killings, as quickly and as quietly as he can. We are to offer him support, as well as ensure that his loyalties to our cause are intact."

Joss swallowed hard. He wasn't certain he was up to the task. Especially with his recent failure with Vlad not that far behind him. But he had to try, had to push past that self-doubt and get the job done. It was the only way to prove his loyalty to the Society. He might not be able to repair his actual family, but his relationship with his Slayer family was something he could mend. He moved his eyes from one Slayer to the next as he spoke, certain not to skip over his uncle. When he spoke, it was with conviction and certainty. "I will fix this. I promise you that."

Morgan took a step closer and growled, but the sadness in his eyes belied his tone. "You'd better, little brother. You'd better."

·5·

THE PLAN

s Joss moved toward the street, Cratian stopped him with a large hand to the chest. "Where, exactly, do you think you're going?"

Joss blinked. He wanted to say that he was going to go look for vampires—particularly any that might be serial killers—but on further thought, that seemed like a pretty stupid reply. So instead, he simply swallowed and stared at Cratian, hoping that he would tell him exactly where it was that he was supposed to be going.

Cratian sighed, reclaiming his hand. "We can't just wander Manhattan, hoping to blindly discover the killer. We need a plan, kid."

"Right. A plan." Joss nodded eagerly.

Cratian crossed his arms in front of his chest and looked expectantly at Joss. "So . . . ? It's your shootin' match. What's the plan?"

Joss's heart sank into the pit of his stomach. Plan? He had no idea what the plan was! Shouldn't someone more experienced with all things plan-making be in charge of this?

As his panic subsided, Joss snuck a pleading glance at Morgan, who, thankfully, knew a cue when he saw one. "Obviously, Joss wants to head to the morgue, so we can examine the body for clues."

Joss gulped. Morgue? Who said anything about a morgue? All of the Slayers were staring at him, waiting for him to respond, to direct them in one manner or another. So he straightened his shoulders and nodded. "Obviously."

Morgan grinned. "Not to mention the body's friends. Right, Joss?"

Joss's eyes went wide. Friends? There was more than one body waiting for them at the—gulp—morgue? "R-r-right. . . ."

Morgan slapped him roughly on the back. "So let's go, little brother. We've got three corpses to examine. The most recent victims of a psychopathic serial killer, all laid out neatly and awaiting your skills as a medical examiner. Lead the way."

Joss's stomach shriveled up into a little ball. He had no idea where the morgue was, or how to get permission to go inside and poke around. And he certainly didn't want to touch one dead body, let alone three! What was Morgan thinking?

After a moment, Paty, Ash, and Cratian chuckled. Then Morgan put a hand around Joss's shoulders and led him away. "Come on, little brother. It's this way."

Joss's stomach was already turning, and they hadn't even opened the door yet. From the outside, the building didn't look like an underground, secret morgue, run by the Slayer Society. Not that he was expecting a neon sign hanging out front or anything, but the outside of the building looked like a deli that hadn't been open in a very long time. In the window was a dust-covered sign that proclaimed the building was available for lease, but Joss imagined that was just for show. The Society did everything they could to make things appear completely normal. That being said, he couldn't help but wonder what they would say or do if a curious realtor or business owner contacted them to inquire about a lease. "Sorry," he imagined them muttering into the phone. "But that property is in secret use. You see, we perform autopsies there on victims of vampires."

Morgan pushed the small, filthy doorbell and

stepped back, saying nothing to Joss. Joss had been hoping he'd speak, that he'd say something to lighten the mood. It was a somber occasion, yes, to go see a body and examine it for clues to a crime. But Joss needed something lighter to ease his stress, something to distract him for a moment. It had been difficult enough to see the man's remains lying in that alley. But to walk into a room and witness his autopsy examination . . . that was seriously stressing Joss out. He'd seen tons of true crime shows and had watched several cop shows with his mom, but there was an enormous difference between television death and real death. Real death was scary. Real death was a taste of the future, a bite of the inevitable.

But Morgan wasn't about to crack a joke to ease Joss's stress. Maybe because he knew that Joss needed to take this seriously. Maybe because he knew that even a small joke wasn't going to erase the fact that they were about to be incredibly close to a dead man. Maybe because he didn't care. Joss didn't know for sure. All he did know was that there was a shuffling noise inside the old deli, and then a figure appeared on the other side of the grimy glass.

Without uttering a single word, Morgan slipped his hand into his shirt pocket and withdrew something, slapping it against the glass for the mysterious figure to see. It was only as he was returning the item to his pocket that Joss realized it was Morgan's Slayer coin. His own Slayer coin was in the left front pocket of his jeans. He mindlessly traced the coin with his thumb as the figure unlocked the door. Before stepping inside, Morgan threw him a glance. "Keep it cool, little brother. Don't think too much about what you're seeing. Just go through the motions, and you'll be okay. In and out. You ready?"

Without thinking—perfect practice for this whole experience, he wagered—Joss nodded and followed Morgan inside.

What greeted him as he moved into the building was dust on dust on more dust, and echoes of what looked as if it had once been a bustling business. The menu board still listed dishes available for hungry customers—everything from sandwiches and fries to soup and salad. Small square tables sat piled at the far end of the room, and beside them were stacks of chairs. If it weren't for the layers of dust and neglect, the furniture would have been bright red in color, matching every fourth tile in the floor. But what had once been filled with voices and movement and delicious, foody smells was now a forgotten place.

Joss's footsteps were nearly soundless on the floor as he followed Morgan to the back of the deli. In front of them, leading the way, was a short, pudgy man. Thanks to Morgan's broad shoulders and impressive height, Joss could barely get a look at him, but what he saw gave Joss the impression that the man was utterly humorless.

They moved swiftly through the dining area and kitchen, and slipped through a small door at the back of what might have been a storage area of some kind. As they descended the stairs wordlessly, Joss felt his heart flutter with uncertainty. He knew for a fact that if Morgan weren't here, he certainly wouldn't be following this strange, unpleasant man into a secret door and down some dusty stairs. But he trusted Morgan—maybe more than he trusted any of the other Slayers—and he knew that Morgan would never lead him into a situation that he couldn't handle.

At the bottom of the stairs was a large metal door with enormous hinges, and when the nameless man opened it, puffs of fog rolled out, giving Joss pause. He'd seen enough crime shows to know that dead bodies were stored inside coolers, but he'd never seen an entire room that *was* a cooler.

Their host grabbed two large coats from hooks on the wall and tossed them to Joss and Morgan. Once the coats were on and zipped closed, he handed them each a pair of rubber gloves and led them inside. "Close that door."

They were the first words he'd uttered to them since they got here.

The inside of the cooler room was lined with steel, all but the floor, which appeared to be solid cement. All along the far wall were metal gurneys, and on top of each was a black bag that was zippered closed.

Joss tucked down deeper inside his coat's collar. He'd seen enough television, enough movies to know what those bags contained. They were body bags, and Joss was here to peer inside of not just one, but three.

Only he didn't know exactly how he felt about that.

On one hand, he'd seen death before, so it was nothing new to him. But on the other . . . two of these bodies had been dead for a while. Long enough to exhibit things like rigor mortis, when a body goes stiff, and livor mortis, when a body turns a weird bluish color. Witnessing the decaying of a body somehow made the death so much more real to Joss. Truth be told, it frightened him to be confronted with death in this way. It scared the hell out of him.

But Slayers don't turn and run. Slayers face their fears.

Their host pulled one gurney to the center of the room and looked pointedly at Morgan, then at Joss. "The one nearest the door just got here. Don't touch any of the equipment. And when you're done, hang those coats back up and make sure you close the door."

Joss sputtered, "We will, sir."

The man paused, as if he wasn't used to being given due respect, and nodded before disappearing out the cooler room door.

Morgan slid his gloves on and Joss followed suit, hoping that he wouldn't have to touch the body at all. Then Morgan looked at him as he stepped over to the gurney farthest from the door. "The first time I came to a Society morgue, your uncle made me open the body bag. He said it was better just to get it over with, to face that fear and move on. He said he was doing me a favor—one that I wouldn't be grateful for until many years later. As it turns out, he was right."

Joss inhaled deeply, which was a mistake. The smell of frigid temps, preservation fluids, and slowly rotting flesh filled his nose and coated his tongue. Joss gagged, clamping his gloved hand over his nose and mouth. It smelled like latex, which was awful, but so much more pleasant than the smell of the morgue's occupants.

Morgan paused, waiting for Joss to recover. Joss could feel the heat of embarrassment crawl up his neck and paint his face red.

"I'm going to spare you that, little brother. I'm not going to make you do anything. The choice of whether or not you pull that zipper and open that body bag is completely and totally up to you. And after it's done, no one needs to know how it all went down, but for you and me. You feel me?"

Joss nodded, and before he could second-guess what he was about to do, he spoke from behind his latex-covered hand. His voice was muffled, but his words still somehow rang clear. "I want to do it. I want to open it, Morgan."

Morgan seemed to gauge him for a moment before nodding. "Okay, then. Open it up. Let's see what we have."

Joss reached out with his free hand and grasped the zipper pull. Only it didn't go anywhere.

He held his breath and tried pulling it with two hands, and after a moment, it gave and the zipper unzipped. Joss practiced breathing lightly, and tried to ignore the smell, which had intensified once the bag was open. For a moment, he thought he was fine. Then he ran to the trash can on the other side of the room and lost his lunch.

When his stomach had settled some, Morgan pulled back the plastic of the body bag, revealing the corpse of a woman in her mid- to late-sixties. Around her neck was a string of pearls that reminded Joss of his aunt Petunia. Her eyes were closed, and from where Joss was standing, she simply appeared to be sleeping.

Like Cecile at her funeral.

"The first thing we want to look at is her wound and determine cause of death. Ahh . . . yeah, I can see it now. Laceration to her throat." He peered over his shoulder at Joss. "You wanna take a look?"

Despite the fact that he really, really didn't want to take a closer look, Joss nodded and moved in. As he did, Morgan gently moved her head to the side. The flesh on her throat had been ripped away. The pearls on that side were tinged with blood. He stared at her corpse for some time, thinking about Cecile. Not frightening, monster Cecile from his nightmares, but real Cecile. The sweet little girl who lay in a small white coffin at the front of the room, looking very much like she was asleep. He wondered if this woman had a family that was missing her, if she had a brother who loved her, the way that he had loved Cecile. The way that he still did.

Morgan had already examined the second body— another victim, this one a black male, not much older than Joss, with a large puncture wound in his chest. Then he opened the third bag, the one containing the gentleman Mason and his team had discovered earlier. "As we already examined this body as a team in the alley earlier, we can assume his cause of death was trauma to the jugular vein, and loss of blood. But there are no guarantees that that's the truth. So we need to check for other injuries, such as a broken back or neck."

Morgan gently lifted the man's head, feeling along the top part of his spine. Then, in a moment that sent Joss's jaw crashing to the floor, Morgan dropped the head back on the table and backed away, cursing loudly. Joss didn't know what to do or say. "What? What is it, Morgan?"

Morgan growled. "His mouth."

Joss looked from Morgan back to the corpse. Apart from hanging open, he didn't notice anything unusual about it at all. All he could offer in response was a blank stare.

"Inside his—its—mouth, kid. Look inside its damn mouth!" Morgan yanked him closer, and Joss peered inside the body's open mouth. Inside, just behind the canine teeth, were small teeth.

No. Tips of teeth. Tips of fangs. The man, the dead creature that they'd found, was a vampire.

· 6 ·

A FAREWELL TO CHILDHOOD

"I don't understand. Why are we even talking about this? I mean, who gives a damn if vampires kill other vampires?" Ash sounded more than a little irritated, and Paty was having a hard time getting anyone to see her point.

"Because the killer may not be a vampire at all, and Elysia won't take that lightly. Innocents could be in serious danger. Plus, even if the killer is a vampire, it has to be completely nuts to attack and kill its own kind. So do we really want to let some crazy vampire wander the streets of New York?" She shook her head at him, in a way that reminded Joss of his aunt Petunia. "No way. Not on my watch."

Joss sighed and sat forward on his spot on the couch. "Paty's right. We can't just let people die, all because of some vampire. We—I—have to find it, and kill it."

Cratian folded his arms in front of his chest. "So where do we start, kid?"

Joss chewed the inside of his cheek for a moment before turning to Morgan. It was a long shot, but anything was worth a shot at this point. "Morgan, you do a lot of recon. I've seen you rifling through papers. Is there a group of vampires that the others listen to, the way we listen to the Society elders?"

Morgan nodded slowly. "There are several groups, or councils, that run things in Elysia, yes."

"Any of them in Manhattan?"

"Very few of them actually live here, but yeah. A couple. Why?"

Joss smiled. "Get their names and whatever info you have on them. If we can track down the leaders, we can learn whatever it is that Elysia knows. And if we can learn that—"

"—we can gather all of their intel on the killings as well." Paty's mouth hung open in surprise and wonder.

Ash cracked a smile. "Kid, you just saved us months

of work. The vamps must know everything that's happened with the killer. We could catch him."

Cratian nodded. "We could kill him."

"I could." Joss eyed them all with the first bit of confidence he'd felt since stepping off that plane at LaGuardia. "I could kill him. And I will."

Morgan returned to the living room an hour later, his arms loaded up with file folders. He passed them out, and Joss flipped open the red one he'd been handed. Inside was a photograph of a young girl, roughly sixteen years of age. And way, smokin' hot—as Henry would have put it.

She reminded him of Kat.

Kat. He wondered where she was now, and if she ever thought about him in a way that didn't call for vengeance. He doubted it very much. He understood, perhaps better than anyone, Kat's driving need for revenge against the person who'd stolen her father away. After all, Joss shared that same drive, those same emotions, when it came to the vampire who'd killed his sister. He couldn't blame her for wanting to kill him. But he did miss her friendship, despite the fact that he worried that she might follow through on her threats. Her text messages oozed hatred, but also, beneath the surface, showed her pain at having lost Sirus. Because of Joss's actions. His insides twisted with guilt and loss that only Kat could understand. He missed Sirus, too, hate it though he did.

Morgan gestured to the file folders. "These are all some pretty high rollers in Vamptopia, but one is particularly nasty. Who drew Em?"

Joss slid the photograph to the side and read three words that gave him pause. SUBJECT'S NAME: EM.

Morgan looked at him and shook his head. "Figures. She'll be a fun one to track, little brother. Cunning, cruel, and not to mention the oldest vampire that we know exists, which means she's crazy strong. Of course, if anybody has a shot at getting close to her, it's you."

Joss blinked. "Why would you say that?"

Paty chuckled, shoving Joss playfully. "Because you're a teenage boy, Joss. Em is trapped in her age. She'll likely gravitate to other teens. Besides . . . you're cute."

There was a distinct pause. One followed by uproarious laughter from Ash, Cratian, and Morgan. When it finally died down, Cratian patted Joss on the back. "And cute is definitely something you want on your Slayer resume, kid."

Joss rolled his eyes and looked down at one of the sheets of paper inside the red folder, the one that listed usual haunts. "Whatever. I'm going to head out to

Toys "Я" Us and then this Obscura place, see if I can dig anything up about Em."

It wasn't long before Ash and Paty decided to start out on their own respective investigations as well. It felt good to start his journey with two other Slayers. If nothing else, it was a little less lonely.

They stepped outside of the brownstone and Joss marveled in the warm air. Paty grabbed him by the sleeve as they reached the sidewalk and tugged him off to the side, where they were met by Ash. "We have to run through a little tutorial before you hit the mean streets, little man. Camouflage, tracking . . . have to touch on them all before you get started."

Joss drew his eyebrows together in mild insult. "But I know that stuff already. Or are you forgetting that grueling summer in the Catskills?"

She shook her head. "Things are different here, Joss. That was a wild environment, out in nature, where you have to hide, move, search in a certain way. This is an urban environment. They're two completely different approaches."

Great. Joss's shoulders slumped some. Back to square one. Back to makeup application and not knowing what the hell he was doing.

Ash patted him roughly on the arm. "Don't get so worked up about it, kid. It's easier in an urban environment. No mascara required."

Paty gawked. "I never made him put on mascara!"

That made Joss smirk, but he was still worried. How was he supposed to hide from vampires in a place with few trees, and track them on concrete sidewalks? It felt like everything that he had learned last year hadn't prepared him for this scenario at all. He couldn't help but feel a little annoyed at having to, basically, start over.

Ash met his eyes, and even though he'd looked angry at what Abraham had revealed to them about Joss taking money to kill a vampire, there was kindness in his gaze now. Understanding, even. "The crowds are your friends. Blend in with them. The vampires will see you, but they'll care less about a skinny kid who's surrounded by people than one who's not. Stay out of empty alleys and places you'll likely find yourself alone. That makes you an easy target, which is the last thing you want."

Paty nodded in agreement. "Dress in dark colors. Bright colors draw attention, and you don't want to stand out in any way. The key in an urban environment—as any environment—is to blend in with the background. The background in a place like New York is busy streets and bustling places."

"And that," Ash remarked as he stepped onto the street, "is all you need to know."

Paty looked from Ash to Joss, a worried crease on

her forehead. "Ash . . . what about the kid? We can't just leave him to his own devices. I mean, we're tracking some of the most powerful vampires in the world, here. And he's barely out of the ninth grade."

Midstreet, Ash turned back and smiled. "I don't see a kid. I only see a Slayer."

Paty released a frustrated sigh. "Be back here by seven tonight, Joss. And whatever you do, don't engage any vamps you come across. Evade and get your butt back here to report. Remember: reconnaissance and planning before action. If you want to live, that is."

A proud smile curled Joss's lips as he moved down the sidewalk, not knowing where he was headed, exactly, confidence aided his stride. Live? Yes. He wanted to live. He was a Slayer. And nothing and no one could change that.

· 7 ·

RECONNAISSANCE

Abraham had been very clear in his instructions to Ash, Paty, and Joss: do as much reconnaissance as they could before the sun set. Get done and get home before the shadows stretch. As the sun was the vampires' enemy, so it was the Slayers' greatest ally. They had to get out, learn what they could about the vampire leaders, and get back to home base before New York City transformed into Vampire City.

New York, it seemed, was not a place to take unnecessary risks when it came to vampires. It was a common area for the beasts, and once the sun had set, no one was really safe. Especially not Slayers.

Joss moved down the street, his nerves jumping at the idea of navigating Manhattan on his own, let alone encountering vampires. He'd studied a map of Manhattan the entire flight here, and had Internet access on his phone, but none of that could set his nerves at ease. The fact remained that he was still a fourteen-year-old boy in an unfamiliar city, full of a million and a half people—some of whom had fangs.

He took a second to get his bearings, wishing all the while that he could sneak back into the house and get his stake—an impossibility, what with Abraham on high alert and none of the Slayers realizing that Joss already had one. It was a strange thing, the idea of being on such a serious mission, armed with a dangerous weapon, headed for one of the largest toy stores on the planet. But Toys "Я" Us in Times Square was one of Em's usual hangouts, so that was precisely where Joss was headed . . . once he consulted his map, of course.

He remembered the cab passing through Midtown on the way from LaGuardia, and once he figured out which way was north, he started walking. It took him about a half hour, but it wasn't long before he was standing in a crowd of people, wondering where on earth Times Square could possibly be. Only then did he lift his gaze and realize that he was standing at its center. Part of him—the part that was just a simple teenage boy—marveled at the enormous neon signs, bright even during the day, and the tourist in him wanted very much to visit the Hershey store and a few of the shops he passed. But Joss pushed that part deep down inside of him and focused on what he'd come here to find: vampires.

It was a strange thing that one of the oldest vampires in existence preferred to hang out at a child's toy store. Did vampires appreciate toys in the same way that humans did? Did they really appreciate anything other than blood? He wasn't so sure. And he doubted very much that there were many vampires in Midtown. It was such a busy place, full of humans who could see them, could see what they were trying to do. Seemed like an easy place for a vamp to get caught. He imagined vampires would visit the area and then get out quickly, like a buffet of tasty food. He wondered briefly if Vlad had ever been to Times Square before— or Sirus, who he'd tried hard not to think of since the day Joss had found blood bags in his refrigerator, the day Joss realized that Sirus was a vampire. He couldn't think about his old friend, couldn't think about the explosion he'd caused that had killed him. And he certainly couldn't think about Kat and the way that things had been left between them. It hurt too much, and he'd had enough pain to deal with without dredging up something that he had no control over. Someday, he had no doubt, Kat would come for him, and for vengeance for her dead father. But until she did, he had to push her out of his mind and focus on the task at hand. Responding to her texts, acknowledging her in any way was just inviting her into his life. He had to ignore her, to focus on what he was doing. And that meant learning all he could about the serial killer that the Society had tasked him with destroying.

He stopped people inside the store—a few employees, but mostly fellow shoppers—and showed them Em's picture, but no one had seen her. Or at least, no one was admitting to having seen her. He stepped outside and glanced around, marveling at all of the people, but sighing just the same. As entertaining as Times Square was, Joss was here on business. His next stop was the strange little antique store called Obscura—that, according to his map, was much closer to the Slayer brownstone. It was practically on its doorstep, at only seven blocks away.

Joss grumbled under his breath. This meant another half-hour walk back to the brownstone. He should have planned better. Just when he was sure he had studied the map of Manhattan well enough, he'd get all turned around again and waste time. Next time, he swore, he'd do better.

As he walked, he thought about how enormous Manhattan was. There was too much ground, too many buildings, too many small places in between and underneath for one Slayer to cover in a single day. It would take Joss years to search it all. And that was just Midtown. And it was also working under the assumption that the killer that he was looking for wouldn't be moving around all that much—a hugely stupid assumption, at that. As if a bloodthirsty monster was just going to sit around and wait for a Slayer to find it. Highly, highly doubtful.

His phone buzzed and, with some reluctance, Joss withdrew it from his pocket. He wasn't certain why he felt the compelling need to read Kat's messages, but he did. Even though they were threatening, with an undertone of sadness, he found them comforting. He missed her, after all. As sick and stupid as it was, he missed having Kat as a friend. She'd been the only friend, besides the Slayers, who hadn't been related to him, or turned out to be a monster.

He flipped it open and read. YOUR MOTHER IS VERY PRETTY. SHE MISSES YOU, YOU KNOW.——K

His throat dried instantly. His heart picked up its pace. How did she know what his mom looked like, or anything else about her? What was she doing, if she was where Joss thought she might be?

Reluctantly, he typed in a message and hit send. ARE YOU AT MY HOUSE, KAT?

There was a brief pause. FRIGHTENING, ISN'T IT? TO THINK THAT SOMEONE COULD BE SO CLOSE TO HARMING

THOSE YOU CARE ABOUT? YES. I WAS AT YOUR HOUSE. SORRY I MISSED YOU.——K

He hurried to send another message, promising himself it would be his last. COME AND GET ME, KAT. IF IT'S ME YOU HAVE A PROBLEM WITH, THEN COME AND GET ME. I'M WAITING FOR YOU. YOU JUST HAVE TO FIND ME FIRST.

Joss hit send, pocketed his phone, and moved down Seventh Avenue at the same pace as many of the tourists, pausing every few minutes to survey his surroundings. It's not like it made him stick out or anything—hundreds of tourists were doing the same thing, only they were pointing up at the buildings or holding up their cameras, not caring that people behind them were just trying to walk. It was annoying, but it really did make it easier for Joss to blend in, and it gave him time to get a good look around and see if there were any noticeable signs of vampiric infiltration. But all Joss could see when he stopped and looked all around were tourists and frustrated-looking people behind those tourists.

Joss continued down Seventh Avenue and took a right on Fourteenth Street. The sounds had changed since he'd wandered away from Times Square. It was already quieter, already more pleasant, less busy. The street still had tons of people on it, but no one was looking aggravated because someone in front of them just couldn't move another step without snapping a picture of the Coca-Cola sign. There were a couple of street vendors, some businessmen, two young mothers pushing strollers that held tiny babies, and people that Joss was certain he'd forget the moment that they passed. The smell of falafel cooking on one of the food carts made Joss's stomach rumble, but he resisted the urge to stop and buy a snack. After all, he wasn't on vacation. He was doing reconnaissance. He was supposed to be on the lookout for any sign of Em or the serial killer, not tasting yummy street food.

The problem was, he was finding a lot more street food than vampires.

A woman in a crisp purple suit walked by, and as she did, she smiled at Joss. The look in her eyes seemed off, as if her smile hadn't quite reached her eyes and she knew it. As he continued down the street, he glanced over his shoulder. The woman had stopped walking and turned around, her eyes locked on Joss. His stomach did a flip-flop, but he wasn't sure what to make of it. She wasn't glaring at him or anything, or even making her way toward him, but for some reason, Joss felt oddly threatened by her presence.

Then his eyes scanned her face, her body, and Joss knew what was going on, and why he felt like this woman despised him, even though they had never met before. She was pale—paler than she appeared to be. He could make out the line of tan foundation on her neck, covering up just how pale she really was. And something in her eyes reminded him of a show that he'd recently watched on the Discovery Channel—one that featured lionesses hunting. She looked hungry. She looked fierce. She was a vampire, and Joss was completely unarmed.

The corner of her mouth trembled a bit in satisfaction, as if she could see the acknowledgment on his face. She couldn't, though. Joss had become a talented actor in recent months, so clearly there was something more to her reaction, something solid in her mind. An affirmation that could only be brought on by knowing precisely what he was thinking. It was as if she was reading his thoughts, like pages in a book. And something in those pages had amused her.

Joss didn't want to turn away, didn't really want to move in any way. All he could picture was a lioness waiting for her prey to make a sudden movement, and then leaping on it, killing it. He tried to push the image from his mind, but it refused to budge. As did the looming knowledge that Joss's stake remained packed in his suitcase back at their base of operations.

At that thought, her lips twisted into a grin. She *was* reading his thoughts. Abraham had taught him that much last summer. Only he hadn't taught Joss any way to block a vampire's telepathic ability. Maybe, Joss thought, because there was no way to do so. The evil glint in her eye said she knew that he was a Slayer. An unarmed Slayer. The upper hand in this confrontation belonged absolutely to her.

Joss mulled over his options for a moment. He was on a street with people, but the population was quickly thinning. Continuing this trek would likely lead him to a place where he'd be completely alone with the vampire woman. At least . . . if he was right about his map directions. He was feeling foolish, and more than a little bit lost. On paper, New York didn't look this big. It was very different in real life.

He thought it was possible that he was heading in the direction of Washington Square Park, but his confidence was suffering a bit. And even if he was right, to do so, he'd have to walk directly past her—something that sent his nerves jumping like crazy. He didn't want to go anywhere near her. What he really wanted to do was run.

Joss furrowed his brow. Run? That hadn't been his thought. He didn't run when he was frightened. He never had—not since he was ten years old. He buckled down and faced what he was frightened of—except in his dreams, except when it was Cecile who was chasing him. That thought, that panicky suggestion that he should take off down the street in terror, hadn't come from his mind at all, and yet he could still hear echoes of it whispering from the far corners of his brain. *Run! Ruuuuuuuun!*

Narrowing his eyes at the woman, Joss realized that the thought was coming from her. She had, somehow and against all reason, put the thought into his mind, and he realized with anger that a person who was less in touch with their usual selves might believe that thought to be theirs. She was capable of mind control, of all things. It both horrified and intrigued him.

It also reminded him of a moment he'd shared with Vlad right before he'd staked him. Inside his mind, he'd distinctly heard the words *StakeVladStake VladStakeVlad* . . . but had they been his thoughts, or something put there by someone—some*thing*—else? By D'Ablo, maybe?

No. Of course not. He was just having a moment of self-doubt. He'd gone to Bathory to stake a vampire. He was just second-guessing those actions now, because the vampire had tricked him into believing they were friends.

Clenching his fists at his sides, Joss strode with a confident step toward the vampire woman. A look of intrigue passed over her features as he approached, but she said nothing. As Joss passed her by, he muttered, "Nice try, bloodsucker."

He walked by, keeping his stride as certain as

he was able, and as he turned back onto Seventh, he glanced in her direction. Only she wasn't alone anymore. Two more vampires stood at her sides, bookending her. They were both male, but one was tall and lanky, the other short and with a stocky build. And all three of them were watching Joss with a noted hunger in their eyes.

Tearing his gaze away, Joss hurried down the street, staying with the crowd for as long as he could. As he navigated his way down the street, the sun began its initial descent, stretching the shadows more quickly than Joss had realized it would. He picked up the pace, and as darkness draped over the city, Joss found himself jogging, then running, then sprinting. Because Ash had warned him not to be out after dark in Manhattan, and he trusted Ash completely. Besides, he could always check out Obscura tomorrow.

As the cool of night enveloped him, the front steps of the brownstone came into view and Joss slowed his running until he was just walking again, his heart still hammering in his chest. In the not too far distance, he swore he heard a voice say, "Sounds delicious."

He hoped that it had been a human that had spoken those words, but couldn't be sure. He hoped it wasn't a vampire that had been eavesdropping on the song of his heart and dreaming about making it its next meal. But he didn't stick around to find out what was what. He hurried up the steps and into the brownstone, his knees aching from all the walking and running he'd been doing today, and closed the door behind him with a loud thud. As he leaned his back against the wood, his fingers reaching for and flipping the dead bolt, his chest rising and falling in uncertain panic, Joss vowed that he would never again come so close to being outside at night while they were in New York. Especially unarmed. Because Ash was right, vampires were everywhere. And you just never knew if they were watching you.

He took a deep breath and let it out, the tension slowly leaving him. As he moved through the foyer, he nodded greetings to Ash, who said, "Hey, kid. Find Em?"

Joss sighed. "Not exactly."

Ash nodded, pursing his lips for a moment. It looked very much like he wanted to say something to help Joss out, but in the end, all he said was, "Morgan's looking for you."

"Thanks." Joss turned and moved down the hall to the library. He'd been hoping for a bit to eat—after all, he hadn't eaten anything at all since the slice of cake earlier, and his stomach was rumbling its protests—but apparently, satiating his hunger would have to wait.

He found Morgan poring over a pile of notes so high that Joss wondered how he could possibly make any sense of it at all.

"What's all this, Morgan?"

Morgan didn't look up. "Intel gathered by our team members. Most of it, I'm sure, is totally useless. Rumored hangouts of the vampire elders. Overheard bits of conversation. Possible relatives. Theories on where they might be located. But it's what we've got. So . . ."

Joss shuffled his feet. He didn't have anything to hand over to Morgan. Hell, he hadn't even known he was supposed to take copious amounts of notes on his activity and findings. It made him feel stupid. It made him feel small.

"Anything to report, little brother?"

Joss shook his head and sighed. "Nothing that lead me to the killer, and there was no sign of Em, but I didn't make it to Obscura. There might be a lead there, I don't know. I'll check it out, though. I did find a few vampires, but the only thing they seemed interested in was having me for lunch."

Morgan looked up at him, a small glimmer of concern in his eyes, but he didn't speak of it. Instead, he nodded slowly and said, "Yeah. They'll do that. Be careful."

Joss lingered there for a minute. He wanted to tell Morgan that he had been careful, and that he had been looking, but he was feeling lost and confused and totally unsure of exactly how he was supposed to track down some serial killer, who may or may not actually be a vampire. But he couldn't say any of those things. And even if he could, Morgan wasn't going to fix this for him, wasn't going to do Joss's homework for him. It was up to Joss to find the killer and dispatch him as quickly and quietly as possible. And he could do it. He was a Slayer, from a long line of Slayers. He could do anything.

So why didn't he feel like he was up to the task?

Without another word, he headed upstairs to the comfort of his bed. Tomorrow, he was going to find a clue if it killed him.

▸ 8 ◂

A VOICE FROM THE PAST

Obscura was a small antiques shop, with lots and lots of things that simultaneously made Joss's skin crawl and thrilled him to no end. There were two-headed animals of the taxidermy variety, human teeth on display, and the creepiest ventriloquist's dummy that Joss had ever seen. It was a weird, wondrous place, full of curiosities that Joss very much wished he could spend time to truly appreciate. But he was here on a mission.

A young man, thin, dressed in a black suit, stood behind the counter, and when Joss said hello, he smiled brightly. "Anything I can help you find?"

"Actually, yes." Joss reached into his back pocket and withdrew the picture of Em. He held it up and the man's face dropped, his skin paling so fast that Joss thought he might just pass out. He knew Em. Clearly, he knew her. And he was terrified of her.

"Do you kn—"

"No." He shook his head at Joss, tearing his gaze away from the photograph. "I've never seen her before. You should look elsewhere."

Joss returned the photo to his pocket. "Look, you obviously know her, so—"

The man met Joss's eyes. "Please. Look somewhere else. I don't want any trouble."

Joss furrowed his brow. He'd scared the man. Simply by showing him a brief glimpse of a photograph. Just who the hell was he looking for that she could inspire that kind of fear? "Okay. Elsewhere. And where might elsewhere be, exactly?"

He hated to scare the man any further, but the fact was, he needed help finding Em, and this guy was one of his only leads.

The man's bottom lip shook. A whisper escaped his lips, seemingly against his will. "You might try V Bar."

Joss put on a pleasant, grateful smile. "Thank you."

As he exited the shop, he heard a distinct sigh of relief from the man behind the counter. It was followed by another sigh from a man on the street.

Joss looked up to see Ash, scratching his head and looking over a crumpled piece of paper in his hands. "Ash?"

At first, Ash blinked at him. Then recognition filled his eyes. "Hey, Joss. Any luck?"

He shrugged casually. "I just got a small lead, so I'm heading over to a café called V Bar to look for Em. What about you?"

"You'd think that finding some big Russian vampire in Manhattan wouldn't be such a challenge. But I got nothin', kid."

Joss furrowed his brow. "Isn't there a huge Russian population here in the city?"

"Yeah. But none that I know of have fangs. At least, I haven't gotten close enough to tell." Ash sighed again and started moving down the sidewalk. "Anyway, I'll catch you later, I guess."

"Later, Ash."

He hated to admit it, but knowing that he wasn't the only one having any trouble gathering intel really made him feel better about his lack of progress.

After a trek that took him several blocks north, Joss entered V Bar, and thought about what had just happened at Obscura. Maybe he should be more careful about flashing Em's picture around town. Maybe people would respond better to his questions. Maybe he'd learn more.

He took a seat at the bar and ordered a black unsweetened ice tea with extra ice. His throat was parched and his feet tired after a long day of recon, so it made him feel relieved that V Bar was somewhere that he could sit down and have a tasty refreshment. The presence of his wooden stake in his back pocket, hidden under his shirt, was an even bigger relief.

Plucking it from his suitcase before breakfast had lifted an enormous weight from his shoulders. It was pretty amazing how comforting just having his stake with him was. Especially considering that he was, to his knowledge, anyway, the only Slayer in the room.

V Bar was an interesting little café. It was also bustling for a late afternoon, but it wasn't so crowded that Joss felt squeezed in or anything. The bartender handed him his tea, took his money, and made change. As Joss dropped three dollars into the tip jar, he said, "This is a cool place. Who owns it?"

The bartender smiled, his eyes sparkling. "My father, actually. A man by the name of Enrico Ciotti. Why do you ask? Are you an associate of his?"

Inside Joss's mind, he weighed the possible outcomes for any given answer. Settling quickly on what he deemed the wisest choice, he nodded. To which, the bartender shook his head, chuckling. "They get younger all the time, I swear. Shall I pour you the house red then? No need to hide behind a tea. The only human here today is pretty drunk in the corner over there."

Understanding spread through Joss's veins like hot lava, slow and simmering. V Bar was owned by a vampire, bartended by a vampire, and frequented by vampires. The man behind the bar was a blood drinker, though likely a young one to be making such blatant slipups like he was, and he now thought that Joss was a vampire as well. In an action so quick and so utterly smooth, the actor in Joss stepped onto the stage and flashed a bemused smile—even though the boy Joss was trembling in terror at the idea that he was currently surrounded by monsters. "Believe it or not," he chuckled. "I actually enjoy the taste of tea."

Smiling, the bartender folded his arms in front of his chest and leaned against the bar. "I've heard stranger things. One vampire I know enjoys jelly doughnuts. Another—a man named Otis—has a distinct weakness for freshly baked chocolate chip cookies."

Joss took a sip of his tea. The hint of fresh mint danced on his tongue, but still his mouth tasted bitter at the mention of a familiar name. He had no real idea of how vast the vampire world was, but Otis, even in the human world, was a relatively unusual name, so he took a breath and let the actor in him inquire. "Do you mean Otis Otis?"

The bartender's expression brightened. "You know him?"

Joss did know Otis. As well as any student knew his teacher. As well as anyone knew their friend's uncle. As well as any Slayer knew a vampire. He sipped his tea again, trying desperately to maintain his calm and casual appearance. "Yeah. I know Otis."

"Then you should meet my father. He and Otis go way back." He gauged Joss for a moment, his smile pursing a bit, as if to say he could read Joss's hesitance in his eyes. "Unless, of course, you and Otis aren't exactly friends."

Joss shrugged. "I'm afraid we had a bit of a falling out in recent times."

Falling out. What a nice way to refer to the fact that Joss had staked Otis's nephew, Vlad, and then Otis had come after him.

No matter where Joss went, it seemed his past was eager to find him.

"A shame. You seem like a nice enough kid." He shook his head, then widened his eyes in apology. "Sorry. I shouldn't call you a kid when I don't know your age."

Joss knew a hint when he heard one. But he really had no realistic idea of how old vampires got. Eighty years? A hundred? Two hundred? A thousand? He had no way of knowing what would be a sensible guess. So he shrugged again and sipped his tea before glancing around the room. To anyone who wasn't in the know, it would look just like any café. The people—the vampires—they just looked so human. So . . . normal. There was no surprise that vampires could blend in so well. "It's okay. No offense taken. So V Bar is usually this busy during the afternoon?"

The bartender refilled Joss's cup and replaced the lid, sliding the cup across the bar. "Depends. Today, as it happens, there's a trial pending, so it's busier than usual. I take it you're not here for that?"

"No. I'm just visiting the city for a bit. Heard it was a pretty interesting place." A vampire to Joss's left lifted a coffee mug to his lips and sipped at the steamy contents. Joss shuddered inwardly at what those contents likely were.

The bartender leaned over the bar, dropping his voice to a conspiring tone. "You're not one of us, are you, kid? You're not . . . a vampire."

It felt as if several hot coals had somehow become lodged in Joss's throat. He swallowed them and they burned all the way down before landing in a heavy pile at the bottom of his stomach. The actor in him had fled the stage, leaving only a panic-stricken Joss behind. He met the bartender's gaze and swallowed, his throat still burning. No words came to mind, nor did any escape his lips to explain what he was and what he was doing here. The realization that he might be on the verge of death settled on the edges of his being like rain on a windowpane. But he shook the thought away. Vampires, he had to keep reminding himself, could read minds. He wasn't even safe inside his own head.

After a moment that seemed to linger for several minutes, the bartender shook his head slowly. "I won't tell if you won't. But you'll find I'm one of the few who can't get a good read on whether someone is human or vampire. Odds are the rest of them know all about you, including your thoughts. So why don't you take your tea and get out of here before you get hurt?"

The burning in his throat lessened some but didn't disappear completely. "I think that's a smart idea."

"Me too." The bartender kept his eyes on Joss as he wiped the bar down with a moist cloth.

Joss bit the inside of his cheek, pinching the soft pink skin between his molars in thought. He wasn't about to bring up Em, but he might be able to get some inside information from a man who talked to everyone about all sorts of things, a bartender. He leaned forward and lowered his voice to a whisper. "Before I go . . . do you know anything about a serial killer on the loose? Maybe a vampire . . . ?"

The bartender groaned and tossed the cloth behind him with a frustrated grunt. Then, inside Joss's brain, he heard a voice. It was clear as crystal, but not at all coming from the bartender's mouth. *"Great. A Slayer."*

The sound jolted him. He knew that vampires could hear humans' thoughts, but he had no idea that it could possibly work the other way around. Doing everything he could to maintain his semi-cool demeanor, Joss raised one shoulder in a noncommittal shrug. "Let's just say I'm a concerned citizen and leave it at that."

The bartender raised his eyebrows in surprise. "You . . . you heard that?"

Slowly, and doubting that he should be admitting to it at all, Joss nodded. He tried to act as if it was no big deal, like he'd listened to a thousand vampires' thoughts in the past week alone. But it was hard to hide his own shock. Why had he been able to hear the bartender's thoughts, and not Vlad's or Otis's? What about this moment was different than those? His heart jumped before settling back into a more normal rhythm.

Wiping his forehead dry with the back of his hand, the bartender moved down the bar and checked on a few other patrons. He poured one a mug of something hot and gave two more cups of half tea, half blood— the vampire's version of an Arnold Palmer. When he came back to Joss, he whispered furiously. "Listen. The only reason I'm telling you this is because my father is forming his own hunting party to take care of the issue. That trial today? It's to make everything nice and legal before my father unleashes his dogs on the city. The whole thing is causing enormous problems for Elysia, risking exposure and endangering our kind. But personally, I think taking action will only expose us further."

Joss listened, waiting for whatever it was that the bartender was trying to share with him. He'd already said a mouthful, but something—instincts, maybe—told him that there was more. "Boris happens to be a personal friend of mine. I've tried talking to him, tried reasoning with him, even tried bribing him, but he's blood drunk, and there's no appealing to his good sense. He's killing just to kill now, and endangering the lives of good vampires everywhere with his senseless acts. I know that only one option remains—taking him down. But my father will rip him to shreds. If you promise me that you'll do it quickly, and as painlessly as possible—and to leave V Bar and never return—I'll tell you where Boris is."

Joss nodded slowly, his heart hammering in his ears. This was exactly what he needed, and he couldn't believe he was getting this information straight from a vampire. He debated whether to share how he'd come across the information with the other Slayers, but decided that would be a bad idea. What if they stormed V Bar? He would have broken a promise to the friendly bartender and possibly endangered his group. No. That was a crazy thought—probably something put there by the vampire bartender. Still . . . some information was safer locked away in his brain.

The bartender searched Joss's eyes, perhaps looking for a modicum of understanding, and then scribbled an address down on a slip of paper. He slid it across the bar. Joss reached for it, but the vampire shook his head curtly, his demeanor shifting abruptly. "Grab it and get out, but act casual and keep your thoughts bland."

Laughter poured into the bar as someone entered behind him. It had a warm, friendly air. "I'll never understand how you can wear that hat in this heat, my friend."

"I love this hat."

Joss straightened. He knew the second voice. It was Otis. Vlad's uncle. From Bathory. Every molecule in his body tightened with tension. If Otis saw him here, he was as good as dead.

The first man spoke again before taking a seat on the stool to Joss's left. "And the girl who gave it to you?"

"You know the answer to that, Enrico." From the sound of it, Otis was standing directly behind Joss. The bartender poured two cups full of a red liquid that sent a wave of queasiness through Joss, then passed them to Enrico, who turned and handed one to Otis. In his peripheral vision, Joss caught a brief glimpse of Otis's sleeve.

"Are you ever going to tell her?"

"I'm fairly certain she knows."

"Fairly certain? Otis, you've just proven the universal truth that no one—not even someone with telepathy—truly understands women."

They both laughed then, and Joss wondered how he was ever going to escape from V Bar unseen.

Apparently, the bartender was wondering the same thing. He moved down the bar some and said, "Otis, it's good to see you again. In town for pleasure?"

"Business. I'm here to assist your father's search." Joss could hear the empathy in Otis's tone—empathy that had not been there the night that Joss had staked Vlad. "I'm sorry, Stephen, I know that you and Boris are close. It shouldn't have come to this, but we have little choice now."

Joss cupped the small piece of paper in his hand and took a sip of his tea. He was just about to casually slide from the bar stool and make his way to the door when a memory flashed through his mind—one that sent a shiver up his spine.

▼   ▼   ▼

On the ground in front of him, Vlad was kneeling, Joss's bloody stake poking out of his chest, the silver tip now stained burgundy. Blood had stained his clothing red, pooling around him on the ground. Vlad's skin was unbearably pale, and as he lifted his head and parted his lips to speak, Joss already regretted the hateful words that he knew would come. He deserved to hear them, yes, but he didn't want to have them echoing in his mind for years to come. What he wanted to do was to cover his ears, his eyes, and run away from this scene as fast as he was able.

He'd just staked his best friend. He'd just killed one of the only people on the planet who cared about him, who he cared about. And the worst part was, he wasn't even sure why. His fingers, slick with Vlad's blood, were trembling.

Vlad tried to speak, but his words could only manage to come out in a whisper. "Joss, behind—"

Then Vlad crumbled over onto the ground. Unconscious. Likely dead—and if not, he would be soon.

Joss turned at his friend's warning to find Jasik, D'Ablo's assistant, he presumed, approaching quickly. He darted a glance to the stake in Vlad's chest, but wasn't sure he could bring himself to remove it. Then, much to Joss's surprise, Jasik gestured behind him. "Do yourself a favor, young one. Get out of here. Now."

Then, in a blur, D'Ablo and Jasik were gone. The

evening played out over and over again in Joss's mind, and confusion enveloped him. Had he really just stabbed his best friend? Had he really just killed the only boy besides Henry to stand by his side? Or was it something else, something to do with D'Ablo? Was D'Ablo—pale-faced and strangely motivated—in fact, one of the undead? Had D'Ablo or Jasik somehow been controlling his actions? Or was Joss now just looking for someone else to blame for the awful thing he'd just done?

Joss's thoughts were racing in panic as he tried to figure out what to do next. Slayer rules dictated that he should immediately contact the disposal unit, followed by his team. But what Joss really wanted to do was to call the hospital and do what he could to help Vlad, even if it meant facing the Society's wrath. Making up his mind to listen to his gut and throw caution and rules to the wind, he reached into his pocket for his cell phone.

But in a blur that reminded Joss only of a strong wind, the phone was knocked from his hand by an unseen force. A moment later, Otis Otis stood in the clearing, inches from Joss, crushing the phone into bits and pieces. His eyes were fierce and fiery. His mouth was curled in a snarl. And in his mouth, his fangs shone brightly. Angrily. Hungrily.

Joss McMillan was about to die.

Otis turned abruptly toward him then, as if the spark of Joss's memory had attracted his attention. Their eyes locked. Otis's voice was quiet, but Joss could feel it coming to a boil just below the surface. "Joss McMillan. Fancy meeting you here."

Joss froze, but offered Otis a polite nod. He couldn't count on his fingers how many times they'd shared the same room, breathed the same air. Otis had seemed harmless then. Just another teacher. Just another man. But he was something else to Joss now. He was the enemy.

Beside Otis, Enrico clucked his tongue. "Enemy? That's a strong word, young Slayer. You'd best be careful who you refer to as such around my fair city. Unless, of course, you're looking to make enemies. Largely by coming here, to my establishment, to cause trouble."

Otis touched a hand to Enrico's chest, as if Enrico had been on the verge of coming at Joss. Only as far as Joss could tell, Enrico had seemed incredibly calm and unmoving. Then, with his eyes still locked on Joss's, Otis spoke to his friend. "There is no trouble here, Enrico, nor desire for trouble. This Slayer, while a skilled adversary, is just a boy. He's not here to cause trouble. Are you, Joss?"

Joss swallowed hard. The actor in him forced a

calm smile. "Not at all. I simply wanted some tea."

"Thirsty, eh? I'm a bit parched myself." Enrico licked his lips. "A positive, are you?"

"Enrico." Otis shook his head. Something about the way he stood—so still, so confident—told Joss that he'd already planned out several ways that he could take Joss's life, if Joss gave him reason to. "Enough."

Slipping from the stool, Joss tightened his grip on the piece of paper in his hand and made his way calmly but quickly to the door. As he stepped outside, his tension eased some, but not much.

Behind him, the door opened again. He fought the urge to break into a run—an urge that was made more immediate by the setting sun. It was about to be dark, and he'd just left a café full of hungry vampires. His Slayer crew, as far as he knew, was halfway across town. Nowhere near close enough for Joss to alert them that he required assistance.

"Joss."

Cursing under his breath, Joss stopped and turned back to Otis, who'd removed his hat. The look in Otis's eyes was serious and meaningful. "I was planning to kill you that night—I would have. But I made a promise to Nelly that I would let you live. If you ever touch my nephew again, I'll take your life. And I will do so with the greatest pleasure imaginable."

Joss swallowed hard before answering. "Thanks.

For not letting Enrico come after me, I mean."

As he returned the purple top hat to his head, Otis said, "It's the last favor I'll ever do for you, Slayer."

"I know." And he did know. Once you'd hurt someone that somebody cared about, there was no asking for forgiveness, and no turning back.

Then, just as Otis was turning back to the door of V Bar, he paused, tilted his hat pleasantly at Joss, and said something that caused the tiny hairs on the back of Joss's neck to stand on end.

He said, "Give my regards to your uncle."

▸ 9 ◂

BORIS

Joss didn't read the bartender's note until he was well away from V Bar. He didn't unfold the slip of paper, or even unclench his fist from around it until he was nearly ten blocks away. When he'd decided he was at last a far enough distance from that place and the vampires gathered there, Joss slowed his steps and opened his hand. The piece of paper that the bartender had handed him was a bit sweaty and semi-crushed, but Joss was very relieved to see that it was still there, that he hadn't dropped it while fleeing or been tricked by some strange vampire power into thinking that he'd been handed a note in the first place. Ever so carefully, as if what he were holding were precious cargo—and, in a way, it was—he unfolded the slip of paper and read over what the bartender had scribbled. In scratchy, hurried handwriting, it read: *Boris—The Bourgeois Pig, 111 East 7th Street, 10:30 p.m.—please try reasoning with him first. Remind him of Cecile.*

Joss's heart sank hard and heavy into the pit of his stomach. Boris somehow knew something about his younger sister. But how? Did Boris kill her? Was he the vampire that Joss had seen the night he'd found Cecile murdered? Or did he know who did it?

And what did some middle-class pig have to do with anything of this?

He folded the paper once again and returned it to his pocket, then withdrew his grandfather's pocket watch and noted the time. He still had another two hours until the time the bartender had mentioned. Until then, he thought it might be a good idea to head back to base and divulge what he knew to the other Slayers. And it might not exactly be a bad idea to arrange some backup. Especially if Boris really was the serial killer they were all hunting. Boris might be dangerous as a psychotic man, but Joss was betting he'd be ten times more dangerous as a psychotic vampire. Nobody, least of all Joss, wanted to face off with some crazy vampire in the dark streets of New York City. Alone.

Yes, he thought, he'd ask the Slayers to help him take Boris down. Then he'd be done with this job, and could get back to . . .

. . . what, exactly? Being the Invisible Boy? Wondering if he would ever avenge his sister's death? Not knowing if he would ever be able to invest himself fully in a friendship again?

Joss stamped his thoughts out like hot embers. There would be time for moping later. Now was a time for action.

As he walked back to the brownstone, his feet aching in Converse shoes—why didn't cool-looking shoes ever have great arch support, anyway?—he thought about Otis. He thought about Vlad. But mostly, he thought about Nelly, and the way that she'd looked the night he'd staked Vlad.

Otis's fangs were out, horrible and gleaming, and Joss knew that he was about to die. "Not yet," Otis seethed. "Not until I make you suffer for what you've done to my nephew."

Joss breathed in, but the air seemed almost too thick with tension to fill his desperate lungs. It was a shame, really, that his final breaths would be those of a drowning man. But Joss was drowning. In fear, in guilt. He didn't know what to say or do to stop this from happening or to explain his actions.

Otis growled, "Don't bother saying anything, Slayer. There's nothing you can do to stop what I'm about to do to you."

In a flash so quick it made Joss's heart stop beating for a moment, Otis moved and was on him like a cat. His hand gripped Joss's hair, pulling Joss's head violently to the side. The heat of Otis's breath on Joss's neck made his bottom lip tremble.

This was it. Now he'd know exactly how his younger sister had felt when that monster had ripped out her life. Now he'd be reunited with Cecile forever.

Otis drew back, narrowing his eyes. "Cecile?"

"He's alive! Otis! Quickly!" Vikas shouted excitedly.

Without even a pause, Otis hurried to his nephew's side. After feeling for a pulse, Otis's shoulders relaxed some. He withdrew a cell phone from his vest pocket and put it to his ear. After a moment, he spoke, his voice troubled. "Nelly, Vlad's been hurt . . . no, badly. Very badly . . . I can save him, but I have to do it now. Can you come get Joss? . . . Just hold him there until I get back . . ."

Joss swallowed hard. His death had merely been postponed.

Then Otis pulled the phone from his ear quickly, as if he'd been hung up on. He looked at Joss as he returned the phone to his pocket. Beside him, Vlad looked dead. "If you move so much as an inch, Slayer, I'll kill you where you stand. Don't even think about running."

And, as much as it might irritate his uncle Abraham, Joss hadn't thought about running. Not once. He'd staked a vampire, yes. But he'd also very nearly killed his best friend, and he had to stay here to see this through. Whether Vlad lived or died determined who Joss was in this scenario: the Slayer or the boy. Both aspects terrified Joss, though he would never admit to it.

He nodded at Otis, and moved his attention back to Vlad, who seemed so lifeless. His chest didn't move. His eyelids didn't flutter. And Joss was very concerned that he might have just succeeded in taking his best friend's life.

And he still wasn't sure why.

He remembered everything about the confrontation in the clearing. He remembered Vlad trying to reason with him in a rather cunning way, and he remembered the undeniable sense of right and duty that had washed over him. He had known that killing Vlad was exactly the right thing to do at the moment, so why now was he filled with such crushing doubt?

In a flash, a very angry Vikas was inches from Joss's stunned face, his fangs out, his eyes furious. "I should rip your skin from your body and wear it like a coat. How could you do this? He is an innocent! He's just a boy, you vile betrayer!"

In the distance, Joss heard a car approach, followed by a slamming car door. None of them moved, waiting for whoever had stumbled on to this grisly scene. Then, out of the darkness ran Nelly, Vlad's guardian. Her eyes were red, her face white, her lips trembling. As she approached Vlad's unmoving body, her shaking hands found her mouth. Otis moved to her to comfort her, but she pushed him away. "That stake has to come out. We need to put pressure on the wound and get him a lot of blood."

The nurse in her was trying to find reason and sense where the mother figure could not. Otis nodded, "Vikas and I will handle it. We have a team of vampire doctors in Stokerton. The ambulance is already on its way with lots of blood. I'd carry him to the hospital, but even though it would be faster, I fear he would bleed out before we reached it."

Nelly's eyes found Joss then and filled with tears that she immediately blinked away. "If you hurt Joss for this, Otis, I will never forgive you."

Otis's expression darkened. "You don't understand, Nelly. The boy is a Slayer. He did this to Vlad."

Nelly's jaw set with a stubbornness that surprised Joss—one that he would have bet that she reserved for special occasions. "I understand more than you could ever know. If Joss did this, he had his reasons. Even if those reasons were ridiculous and wrong. I won't have more blood spilled. Leave him alone."

Otis and Vikas exchanged looks. Nelly said, "Joss, come with me. We'll get you cleaned up before I go to the hospital."

But she didn't mean "cleaned up." Joss could tell by the inflection in her voice, by the look in her eyes. She meant "safe," away from the vampires, someplace where no one could hurt him. Nelly was willing to put off racing to the hospital with her nephew in order to protect a boy she hardly knew. Or did she know Joss? He'd spent countless hours at her house. And every time, she'd welcomed him in with open arms. Was that because she understood him as a person? Joss didn't know. All he did know was that in a moment when he desperately wished for his mother, Nelly was here to help him. She nodded toward the car. "Come on. Let's go home."

As they walked away from the clearing, away from Vlad, Joss's shoulders sagged. His heart felt as heavy as the guilt it held. He swallowed hard, trying to push down the hurt. Nelly put an arm around him and gave him a squeeze. "It'll be okay, Joss. I promise. Every-thing will be okay."

▼　　▼　　▼

The lights were on at the brownstone, and Joss had planned on going inside, but he didn't think it was such a great idea to face his uncle when he was struggling with the sheer, unending regret of having staked his best friend. His steps slowed in front of the brownstone. Wait. No. He'd staked a vampire, who just happened to be his best friend. Or had been his best friend—past tense. Wasn't that more fitting? Were he and Vlad still friends after what had transpired? After Vlad had betrayed him and he had betrayed Vlad in kind? Had they ever been friends? Had their friendship been truly genuine? Or was the entire thing just a clever vampire ruse? A way of keeping the Slayer at bay and under control?

Joss had no way of knowing. And he was quite certain that he'd never know, that he'd never again return to Bathory—though he very much wished that he could. If for nothing else than to right the wrong that had transpired between him and Henry.

He hadn't seen his cousin before leaving town, but that was largely because Joss had avoided any contact with Henry. He didn't know what to say, and wasn't sure that Henry would have wanted to hear it anyway. So he'd written a note to Vlad, hastily placed it on his locker, and headed outside, where the cab was waiting to drive him to Stokerton International Airport. The note had read "friendship over," but now Joss was wondering if that were true, or if the actor in him had taken over then, too, blinding Joss with his dramatics. It was hard to tell. It was also sometimes impossible to distinguish between Joss the actor, Joss the Slayer, and Joss the boy. Sometimes he felt like his personality was fracturing into a million pieces, into a million people, and he didn't know how to stop it. Or if he really wanted to at all. It was exciting and terrifying. It was life. And it was his, good or bad.

He made his way toward the brownstone's steps in the growing darkness, listening to whispers coming from the shadows within shadows. Part of him wondered if a vampire might leap out of the darkness and end his torment, reuniting him with the sister who he hadn't saved. It frightened him. And in a dark way that he'd never admit to, it intrigued him. He only hoped that the Cecile he'd been reunited with would be the sweet little girl that he'd known and loved, not the terrifying creature from his tormenting nightmares.

Cecile.

He flipped through the pages of his memories back to the moment that Otis had been about to rip his throat out. Otis had said his sister's name in surprise, as if he'd known her personally. But that was impossible, wasn't it? Unless . . .

Joss's stomach clenched.

Unless Otis had killed Cecile, or knew who had.

Inside his jeans pocket, Joss's cell phone buzzed to life. With a deep breath, he pulled it out, hit the button, and put it to his ear. "Joss here."

It was Morgan's voice on the other end. "Better head home soon, little brother. Everything okay out there?"

Apart from the fact that he had no idea how he was going to solve all of his problems, yes, everything was fine. Peachy keen, jelly bean, as his mom would say. Or used to say before he'd lost her to the fog.

"I'm fine. Heading in now." He didn't wait for Morgan to respond before hitting END and returning the phone to his pocket. He was fine. And he didn't need anybody to check on him to make sure. He was strong. He was tough. He was a Slayer.

Before he could second-guess his actions, Joss moved up the steps of the brownstone and through the front door, ready to report. Just inside, he found Cratian standing guard. He nodded a hello before moving down the hall to the living room, where Uncle Abraham was reading a well-worn book in an easy chair near the window. As Joss entered the room, Abraham snapped the book closed and looked up at him. "Report."

Joss took a breath and blew it out slowly, straightening his shoulders in mock-confidence. "I've got a lead."

Abraham's eyebrows raised in surprised disbelief. "Oh? Anything tangible?"

To this, Joss held up the crumbled slip of paper in his hand. "The bartender at V Bar is good friends with a vampire who's been killing humans out in the open. According to him, this vampire is about to be hunted and tortured for his crimes . . . unless we get to him first and dispatch him quickly. He hangs out at a place called The Bourgeois Pig every night at ten thirty."

Abraham took this all in, then opened his book and flipped to the page he'd been reading. Without looking back at his nephew, he said, "Well, then. You'd better hurry. It's getting late."

Joss paused in confusion. "Should I . . . assemble a team or go it alone?"

Abraham glanced up at him. "Do you need a team? As Cratian said before, it's your shootin' match, yes?"

It was a test. His uncle wanted to know whether or not he was capable of deciding what action needed to be taken, and of handling such a task on his own. But as much as Joss wanted to pass that test and strut out the door to engage a monster and impress the Slayer Society—not to mention his uncle—his knees betrayed him by trembling slightly. He was scared, and there was no easy, tough, manly way to admit that he was scared.

What would Abraham do or say if Joss admitted to

feeling frightened? Would he embrace his nephew, tell him everything would be okay, send out Morgan or Ash to handle the big, bad vampire for him? No. Abraham would punish him, and rightly so. Because this wasn't about being a frightened child. This was about being a Slayer, and doing everything that he could to ensure the protection of his fellow men.

With a tightened jaw, Joss turned from his uncle and headed for the door. "Don't wait up."

He imagined Abraham cracking a small, proud smile. But he didn't dare turn back to look.

With determined steps, he made his way to 111 East 7th Street, and tilted his head with interest at the hot spot known only as The Bourgeois Pig. The man standing outside checking IDs gave Joss a brief once-over before waving him through the door, much to Joss's surprise. He had hit a rather extreme growth spurt recently, his height growing dramatically and his shoulders broadening. But he hadn't expected to not even get carded. Without complaint or questioning, he stepped inside and was instantly transported back in time to an old bordello, a thought that might have made him blush if it weren't for the red lights filling the posh space. The walls were covered in brocade, the room filled with gilded mirrors and plush antique armchairs. It was a private place, an intimate place, but one that struck Joss with such extravagance that he immediately felt underdressed in his black skinny jeans and Buffy the Vampire Slayer T-shirt that read I'M THE SLAYER. ASK ME HOW! Abraham hated the shirt, so Joss had made certain to wear a short-sleeved button-up over it, just in case he needed to appease his uncle by covering it up. Joss had thought it was funny and ironic. So had Morgan. And Paty. So at least he wasn't alone.

The room smelled like lavender, and Joss couldn't be certain, but he thought that the scent might be coming from several of the glasses in the room. Glasses that were held, Joss couldn't help but notice, by mostly women. Impeccably dressed, attractive women. In their twenties. Henry would have been in heaven. Joss moved to an empty chair and glanced at the menu, but stopped reading after something called "smelly potatoes." He looked at his phone for the time and noted that it was precisely 10:28 P.M. No sign of Boris so far. Unless he was in drag and very pretty, sipping something that smelled a lot like Joss's mom's bath salts.

How long was Joss going to sit here? He wasn't even sure what Boris looked like. Strike that. He hadn't the slightest clue what Boris looked like at all. How was he supposed to recognize the monster? How long was he going to wait, and how long was he going to go on believing that the vampire bartender hadn't simply sent him on a wild goose chase? Or, worse, set him up to be taken down by other vampires? He looked around at the women in the room, none of whom seemed to notice his presence at all. Could they be vampires? Maybe. They were attractive. Many were pale and fashionable. But how much of that was vampire and how much of it was simply fashion? He couldn't be sure. All he knew is that he'd come here because a vampire had told him to, and he'd believed that vampire. Joss. Duped again by the undead. Hadn't Sirus been enough? Hadn't Vlad? What was wrong with him? What was he thinking?

He stood up, glancing at his phone one last time. Ten thirty P.M. on the nose.

The door opened and a rather elegant gentleman walked inside, a smile on his face. His skin was golden brown, his eyes so dark they appeared black. He wore an ascot around his neck, but did not look at all dorky like Fred from Scooby-Doo. His was different. His spoke of another era. Another time. One from which pages this man, this creature, had stepped directly out of. Joss slipped the phone back into his pocket but remained standing. He couldn't explain it, but he had an overwhelming sensation that this man, this creature, was not only a vampire, but the vampire that he'd been waiting for. With his eyes locked on his mark, Joss thought his target's name—hoping that the creature was listening with its telepathy and would pick up on the single word that burned in his mind.

Boris.

Immediately, Boris turned his head toward Joss, and with a slight twitch in his smile, nodded. Joss waited a moment, then sat down again to wait. Boris approached the bar, saying his hellos as he moved. Clearly, this was a regular stop for him. The women lavished him with attention, and the bartender already knew what drink to have waiting once he got there. After several minutes of social pleasantries, Boris made his way back through the room and took the plush Queen Anne–style chair across from Joss, as if they were old friends. "Can I get you anything to drink?"

Joss shook his head, keeping his expression pleasant. He'd promised Stephen that he would try to reason with his friend, and Joss intended on keeping that promise. "No, thanks. The smell of lavender isn't very appealing to me. Reminds me of bath salts."

Boris chuckled and held his glass up to Joss in a toasting gesture before taking a sip. The contents were red, and Joss wondered if it were an effect of the lights, or the contents themselves. After Boris had swallowed, he swished the liquid slightly, watching his drink move about in the glass before speaking again. Joss did everything he could to keep his thoughts far away from the stake in his back belt loop. It was surprisingly easy. "Not many know my true name outside of Elysia. Would you mind telling me how you came about this privilege?"

Joss kept an eye on the other people in the room with his peripheral vision. He still didn't trust that this wasn't a vampire hangout. "I met a friend of yours at V Bar earlier today. Stephen? He told me."

"V Bar." Boris raised an eyebrow. "Why would a human who clearly has knowledge of Elysia choose to socialize in such a well-known vampire location? Unless you were somehow involved in the trial?"

Joss shook his head earnestly. "I wasn't there for that."

"So why were you there? Unless . . ." He widened his eyes for just a moment and then chuckled, taking another sip of the red concoction. Joss swallowed, straining to keep his thoughts away from his fear that Boris would discover that he was a Slayer before Joss was ready for him to. Then Boris set his half-empty glass on the table between them and spoke again. This time, Joss had the feeling that the words weren't intended for Joss, but for Boris himself, perhaps to ease his mind. "But you're too young to be a killer, now aren't you, boy?"

Feeling slightly more at ease, Joss relaxed a bit, but stayed on high alert. Just in case Boris wasn't above attacking and killing him in such a public space. After all, wasn't that what the serial killer had been doing that had so upset both the Slayer Society and the vampires themselves? Joss pushed that thought away and met Boris's gaze. "Stephen sent me to talk to you about something. He's very concerned that his father and the other"—Joss swallowed the word vampires in case any other humans were listening—"the *others* will hurt you."

Boris's smile lost some of its honesty then. He shook his head, reaching again for his glass. Joss wondered if the glass acted like a kind of security blanket for him, or if Boris really needed a drink. "Oh, he needn't be concerned with that."

"He seems to think so." But looking into Boris's eyes, Joss could see something there—something that spoke of an unshared detail. He tilted his head slightly, curiously as he spoke—the idea that he was purposefully engaging in meaningful conversation with a fanged killer never far from his thoughts, but carefully tucked away inside his head. "Why not?"

Boris gauged him for a moment. Then he drained his glass and returned it to the table once more, this time empty. Not so much as a drop of liquid clung to the depths of the glass. "Because they won't hurt me. They'll kill me."

He could sense the moment approaching, like a

magician getting ready for the big reveal. It was coming. He just had to control when and how. "He seems most concerned that they'll hurt you first. Badly, if I'm judging his tone right."

"And you'll . . . what? *Just* kill me?" Boris threw his head back in laughter.

Joss paused, then thought about his wooden stake. What it looked like. How it felt in his hand. The heft and sincerity of the weapon itself.

Boris stopped laughing. "A Slayer. Ahh . . . I should have known."

Joss nodded, but said nothing. Thought nothing.

"Where's your stake, Slayer?" Boris's words sounded calm, but the edges were furled with an almost unnoticeable concern.

In reply, Joss thought about Scooby-Doo and the way that Fred's ascot looked in comparison to Boris's. He wouldn't give away any details. Not until he was ready for Boris to know them. He might not be able to keep the vampire from reading his thoughts, but he could certainly control what thoughts he had when the vampire was around.

A waitress passed and Boris barked, "Another."

As the two waited for Boris's second drink to arrive, Joss watched the vampire, who seemed utterly perplexed that Joss was doing so well at keeping his thoughts away from his stake. Frankly, Joss was surprised, too. But he had other things to think about. Like a certain name that had been scribbled on a certain piece of paper.

Once Boris had a new drink and had taken a healthy sip, Joss reached into his pocket and retrieved Stephen's note. He unfolded it and set it on the table. "Tell me, Boris. Tell me all about how you know Cecile."

Surprise filled Boris's eyes at the mention of her name, followed by guilt. Joss bristled, hoping that Boris was still listening to his thoughts. If this creature, this monster, was the one that had taken Cecile's life that night, it would wish that vampires were taking it down. Joss would make Boris hurt more than any being had ever experienced pain. And he wouldn't feel an ounce of guilt for any of it.

Boris set his glass down, fingers trembling some. When he spoke, his voice had changed. He seemed shaken. Sad. Guilty.

Joss stiffened, his thoughts turning at once to the stake in his back belt loop, despite the fact that he was desperately trying not to think about precisely that.

Boris's eyes widened briefly, and Joss knew that he'd just revealed the location of his weapon. But it didn't matter. What mattered was Cecile.

"We were close—very close—for just thirteen

years. Until I learned she had ties to the Slayer Society. How do you know of her?"

Joss furrowed his brow. What was Boris talking about? His sister was just a tiny young thing when she'd died. Cecile was barely in elementary when her life was stolen from her, when she was stolen away from Joss.

Boris's eyebrows came together then and he shook his head. "We're speaking of two different Cecile's, Slayer. Your Cecile was a child, an innocent who was murdered in her sleep. My Cecile was a beautiful woman, who fell in love with two men and had to choose between them. She chose, to my heartbreak, the other man."

Cecile. Of course! Joss felt only slightly stupid when he'd realized that the Cecile who Boris was talking about had been Ernst's first love, the woman after whom his sister, Cecile, had been named. Joss's head swam. How could this be? He'd been so close to information about who had killed Cecile. He was so certain! And now . . .

Boris shook his head, returning to his crimson drink. "Curse you, Blomberg."

A jolt went through Joss, and he sat bolt upright in his seat, eyes on his conversational companion. "Blomberg? Ernst Blomberg?"

Boris nearly dropped his glass before returning it to the table once again. "How did you know?"

Joss set his jaw. His heart had picked up its pace, and his entire body felt as if it were on high alert as the adrenaline rushed through him. The reveal, he'd thought, would have been the location of his stake, but Joss was mistaken. The big reveal in this magician's act was about to occur. He locked eyes with Boris, took a steady, calm breath, and said, "I haven't properly introduced myself, Boris. My name is Joss McMillan. I'm the great-great-great-grandson of Professor Ernst Blomberg."

A fiery, hate-filled glare flashed through Boris's eyes then, and he growled low enough that no one else in the room would hear. "Well, then, Joss McMillan. It will be my immense pleasure to watch you die."

· 10 ·

ANY PORT IN A STORM

Joss didn't have time to think—not that thinking would have been wise at that moment. What he needed was to rely purely on his Slayer instincts— they were the only thing, after all, that might help him get out of this alive.

Boris lunged at him, sending his glass flying, its liquid contents spilling out in slow motion droplets that momentarily decorated the air to Joss's right. Joss dove to the left, landing on the floor just as Boris connected with his newly emptied chair, toppling it over and landing in a heap. Joss scrambled to his feet, ignoring the screams and gasps from his fellow patrons, and reached for his stake, gripping the wood tightly in his hand. Boris roared and, before Joss could even blink, the vampire rushed him, slamming Joss against the door. His fangs were long and sharp. His breath smelled sickly like blood. It reminded him of the vampire who'd killed Cecile.

Joss whipped his arm up and over, catching Boris's shoulder with the tip of his stake. Boris cried out. "You will die, Slayer!"

He slammed Joss against the door again. Pain ripped quickly through Joss's spine, and for a moment, he saw stars. Only the stars didn't disappear. In a blink, Joss realized that Boris had ripped the door from its hinges. He was lying outside, with a seriously ticked off vampire pinning him to the ground.

Joss blocked out all thought and did what his instincts told him to do. He kneed Boris in the groin.

Joss rolled free and moved to the nearest shadows, hoping to conceal himself briefly. Just until he'd formulated a plan to take Boris down. He stood in the alley nearest The Bourgeois Pig, stake in his fist, and waited for Boris to move after him and claim his vengeance with both fangs.

Boris bared his teeth, his fangs elongating once again—slowly, this time—and stood. Joss could have sworn that he heard a low growl emanating from his adversary, even at this distance. "Cecile was my soul mate, Slayer. Your family broke that bond, and for that, you must die."

Joss very much wanted to point out that, in theory, a bond between souls couldn't be broken. A bond was forever. So perhaps Boris had been wrong about the connection he and Joss's great-great-great-grandmother had shared. Maybe it had been more of a crush-type situation than undying love. After all, their love had died. Hadn't it? At least Cecile's half.

But he said nothing. There was a task at hand, and chitchat wasn't going to get it done any faster. Joss just hoped that he was up to it. Boris was muscular, and even the weakest vampires were incredibly strong. But Joss didn't have much choice in the matter. This fight was going to happen with or without his consent.

And yet, he found himself standing there, not acting, not moving forward to engage Boris. Why? Because he sympathized with a fellow living creature?

No.

Because Boris was putting something in Joss's brain, in his thoughts. Boris was making him doubt his own motives and hesitate to make the first move. And if a vampire was capable of controlling thought and motivation, what else might it be capable of?

Slowly, with a knowing smirk on his face, Boris removed his jacket and ascot, and folded them neatly.

He piled them on the ground near the wall, stood, and cracked his neck—first to the left side, then to the right. Joss watched him, wondering what he was thinking, what anyone might think before they attempted to kill a boy his age. Was he anxious to begin?

"More anxious than you could ever know," Boris spat at him before disappearing in a blur. Joss squeezed the stake nervously in his fist, but he couldn't see Boris anywhere, and felt only the mildest of breezes on his right side. His hair ruffled, but only slightly. If Joss didn't know better, he'd have said that Boris was gone.

But Joss did know better. He knew that vampires were ultrafast and sneaky, and absolutely could not be trusted. He narrowed his eyes, turning slowly, trying to distinguish Boris from the shadows around him. All he found was darkness.

From his left came a hushed echo of laughter. Joss turned, but no one was there.

He didn't like this. He didn't like games. And he didn't like being toyed with. "Come on, Boris," he whispered into the night air—air that suddenly felt chilly. "Come out and fight like a man."

A sudden breeze brushed his left side and then Boris was there, hand on Joss's throat, squeezing. His fangs gleamed, even in the low light, as he growled into Joss's face. "And what would you know of fighting like a man, Joss McMillan? You're just a boy. You know nothing."

Joss swallowed against Boris's grip, his heart betraying his cool exterior by beginning to race. Acutely aware of the wooden stake in his hand, he hissed. "I know one thing. I know how to kill your kind."

Boris chuckled. "Oh, really? Why don't you tell that fairy tale to the vampire who killed your darling sister?"

Joss yanked his arm back in fury, but Boris caught it effortlessly with his free hand and held it still. "You think about her enough—it comes off you like a heat, that want of vengeance—but what have you done ever since developing your Slayer skills to hunt down her killer? You're a waste of time and space, like any Slayer, like any human."

Joss spat at him, "Like Ernst's Cecile?"

Boris's hand clenched Joss's throat. The air was choked off, and suddenly, unexpectedly, Joss saw stars. Boris's words grew faint and the world began to turn in on itself. "Never speak ill of my Cecile."

Boris released his grip and Joss coughed, the world turning right again. The stars remained for a moment, but quickly turned into spots that faded with every breath. Boris was toying with Joss, trying to draw out the kill, like any sadistic serial killer would. Slowly,

Boris pressed the tip of his thumb into Joss's wrist. After a moment, his fingers tingled with numbness. Joss struggled uselessly. He kicked, but couldn't seem to connect. Maybe he'd been weakened by the brief lack of oxygen, he couldn't be certain. But there was no escaping Boris for the moment, no matter how he tried. After another moment, his hand opened, dropping the stake to the concrete below. The sound that the wooden weapon made as it hit the ground reverberated through Joss's entire being. He was unarmed. And at the complete mercy of an angry, vengeful vampire.

Boris grinned, but there was no joy in it—only an undying fury that burned like embers in his skull. He gripped Joss's throat tighter and then, to Joss's utter shock, they were flying upward. His feet left the ground, floating high above where his abandoned stake now lay. The bricks of the building across the alley flew by in a blur as they rose through the air. And when they stopped, Boris slammed Joss's back against the bricks of the building behind him. The stars returned for a second, and then the back of Joss's head felt moist. Dazed, he tried to focus his vision on anything but Boris.

Across the alley, a window was open, its peeling frame propped open by a rusty screwdriver. The lights were off, and Joss knew that no one was at home. No one could help him now. No one would save him. He was going to die in an alley, and no one—not even his fellow Slayers—would know that it was a vampire that had killed him.

Boris sniffed the air, smelling Joss's blood. "I have decided, Joss McMillan, that I will bring you to the brink of death, and finish the task by draining you dry. That way you'll understand exactly how your darling sister felt in her final moments, as the life ebbed from her body, aided by your cowardice."

Joss opened his mouth to curse his attacker, but his words were struck from his mind the moment that Boris released his grip. Joss dropped like a stone, falling through the night air so quickly that he barely had time to comprehend what was transpiring. Then, as the ground neared, time slowed some, and Joss's thoughts were consumed with mental photographs of those he cared about and how very much he was going to miss them. His grief was choked off by Boris's familiar grip on his throat once more.

They flew upward again, but the brief sense of relief that had filled Joss quickly dissipated. He was nothing more than a plaything now, a delicious rag doll, ripe for the biting. Boris slammed him against the opposite building this time, and Joss managed a groan of pain. His head ached. The blood on the back on his head had just begun to become sticky, but as Boris slammed him against the bricks again, the wound broke open, pouring blood down the back of Joss's neck. The muscles in his back were screaming.

Boris grinned—a meaningful, happy grin at last—and spoke to Joss in a voice that dripped with patronizing syllables. "Children should stay at home, mind their manners, and leave the real world to the adults. And you, Joss McMillan, are a child. Stupid, selfish, and out of your league."

Joss's mind felt full of fog, but something danced on the edges of his thoughts, something he was struggling to grasp with each word that Boris spoke.

Boris's mouth opened wide, and he lunged forward. Joss couldn't see what he was doing, but felt it instantly. Boris's fangs sank deep into his neck, filling him with an immediate pain. Joss struggled but couldn't break free. Boris held him close, drinking deep, and just as Joss's eyelids threatened to flutter close and surrender to the dizzying moments before his death, the memory that he'd been struggling to recall became clear, almost crisp in his foggy brain.

Joss turned his head slightly to the right and found what it was that he'd been thinking of. He stretched his trembling hand out and gripped the rusty screwdriver. Joss yanked the tool free, the window slamming closed without it. His mind echoed three simple words— words that he could not speak aloud. *"For you, Cecile."*

With all his might, Joss stabbed the pointy end of the screwdriver into Boris's back. Boris howled and thrashed, releasing his jaw from Joss's throat.

And then they were falling.

Joss didn't have time to think about what would happen when they hit the ground. He merely held onto Boris, clutching the vampire to him in absolute terror.

Boris hit the ground first. The screwdriver plunged through his back, bursting through his chest with a spatter of blood. The blood bloomed out all around him on the concrete. Joss sat on top of his corpse, eyes wide, heart racing, neck still bleeding. Quickly, as soon as he could grasp his reason, he stood and plucked Boris's ascot from the ground, pressing it tightly to his neck with shaking fingers. Then he picked up his stake and slipped it through his back belt loop.

From his pocket, he withdrew his cell phone and pressed number two on speed dial. When the mysterious voice on the other end answered, he said, "This is Joss. I need a cleanup in an alley near One Eleven East Seventh Street, Manhattan. No pickup."

His throat burned as he spoke, his words coming out in strangled whispers, no matter how much he forced them to sound normal. When the voice replied, "That's a go, Joss. Cleanup crew is on its way," he hung up and returned the phone to his pocket.

He didn't look back as he exited the alley. And he wasn't at all certain how he managed to find his way back to base. But the moment he staggered in the front door, he was relieved to be home.

He collapsed in the foyer, and Paty was on him in seconds, helping him to stand, ordering Ash to grab the medical kit, telling Morgan to get his bed ready. Cratian lifted him up, and as they turned to go to Joss's bedroom, Joss saw his uncle Abraham. "Did you kill it, nephew? Did you kill the vampire? Did you take down the serial killer?"

Joss's words were barely a whisper. It was all that he could manage. "I did."

Abraham breathed out a slow sigh of relief, one that Joss was so grateful to hear.

Then the colors of the room swirled together. Darkness swallowed him whole.

· 11 ·

COLORING WITH CECILE

Joss opened his eyes—not after sleep, but after what felt like an extended blink—and realized that he was standing in an alley, in some city. Maybe it was New York. Maybe Chicago, or Detroit. He couldn't be sure. He only knew that the smell of fresh tar mixed with exhaust and decay filled his nostrils, and the scene around him was hard, gray, and cold. His feet stood on cracked cement, and the walls that lined the alley were composed of bricks and mortar that had seen better days. It was a forgotten place, this alley, and Joss had no idea what compelled him to move deeper into it and turn the corner at the end. But he followed his instinct, despite the tightening of his chest and the tiny hairs sticking up on the back of his neck.

The alley, which ended in a dead end after the turn, was empty. Joss narrowed his gaze, peeking back over his shoulder. It wasn't supposed to be empty. Was it?

A humming reaching his ears, a little girl's wordless song. It was coming from the dead end. Joss turned back, facing it. There, at the end of the alley, was Cecile. She was on her knees, tiny hand clutching an over-sized piece of pink sidewalk chalk. As she drew the chalk across the cement, it crumbled slightly, leaving behind a crooked pink line—one that reminded Joss of another line . . . one that he swore had run from the corner of someone's mouth down to the sheets. But as soon as the thought, the memory, had entered his mind, it was gone again. He remained where he was, watching his younger sister drawing lines in the alley for several minutes before speaking. Maybe he didn't want to disturb her serenity. Or maybe, another fleeting thought whispered into his mind, he was afraid of her.

Cecile stopped humming for a moment and straightened her shoulders. She didn't turn to face him, but Joss knew that she was aware of his presence. As if in response to that knowledge, his heart picked up its pace. Without looking at him, Cecile stretched out her hand and pointed to the small bucket of chalk a few feet to her left. He watched her hand carefully, a worry filling him that her nails would somehow become claws. But this was his sister. He loved her. He had nothing to fear. Besides, she was just a child, and he was a fierce killing machine. Certainly, he could defend himself if Cecile . . .

Joss shook his head, chasing those delusions away. This was his baby sister. He had nothing to be afraid of, nothing to defend himself against. She was a child. A sweet, innocent child. "Do you want a different color, Cecile?"

She tapped her finger wordlessly at the bucket again. With a deep breath, Joss stepped forward and crouched beside his sister. "What about blue? Blue's nice, right?"

When she didn't respond, he plucked a piece of blue chalk from the bucket and placed it in her hand. She gripped it and immediately went back to drawing. Joss watched her profile for a while as she colored. Her hair hung in her face, and he had to fight the urge to sweep some of her curls back over her ear so that he could see her eyes. After a while, he said, "What are you drawing, Cecile?"

But Cecile didn't reply. She merely stopped the chalk from moving and abruptly set it on the cement, as if indicating that her creation was finished.

Joss turned his head slowly and looked at what

his sister had created. In bright, happy colors, a crude, childlike design showed a vampire lying dead on the ground, a screwdriver sticking out of his back. Beside the vampire lay a small girl, fang marks in her neck, her eyes wide open and lifeless. Above both of the corpses stood a boy. The drawing was crude, but the boy was obviously Joss. When Joss found his voice, it was in whispers. "Why would you draw this, Cecile?"

Cecile retrieved some chalk and began drawing on another section of pavement, but Joss's eyes were locked on her first creation. Though drawn in that messy way that only a child can make look charming, the faces were incredibly expressive. The vampire and the girl looked as if they'd died horrifically, and the scribbled Joss character stood there without remorse. Joss's chest felt suddenly hollow. Is that how she felt? That he had no remorse in his slaying of Boris? That he had no guilt at all for not stopping her demise?

How could she want him to have remorse for killing that monster, that beast, when it was a vampire who'd taken her young life? No. He wouldn't feel guilty, despite whatever images his twisted subconscious dredged up.

Cecile finished her furious scribblings and tossed the chalk on the ground, shattering it. Joss turned his head at her abrupt movement and looked at what she'd drawn.

A crudely drawn boy lay across a small, blond girl's lap. Their features were hurried and not unlike stick figures, as if she'd had to draw them as fast as possible. As if the message she wished to convey to him could no longer wait, could no longer be contained. The boy's eyes were wide and terrified, his mouth contorted in a scream. In the girl's chalk hand was a bouquet of poorly drawn flowers, mostly tulips and daisies. Her eyes were swirls of black, layers and layers of chalk that made the cement they were drawn on disappear completely beneath. Her mouth was large and open wide. Inside were two fangs, dripping with blood.

Only the blood hadn't been drawn in chalk.

The deep crimson dripped from chalk Cecile's mouth onto chalk Joss, quickly pooling on the cement, washing away the drawing. The blood oozed closer and closer to where Joss was kneeling, and he scrambled to get to his feet.

But then a hand—clawed and filthy—wrapped around his wrist. Cecile turned her head very slowly toward him. As she moved, the pool of blood soaked into his jeans. His heart hammered inside his chest and that voice that had whispered his fears as he entered the alley screamed out its told-you-so inside his brain. By the time Cecile's black, soulless, tunnel eyes met with Joss's terrified gaze, he was in full on panic mode, shaking his arm, trying to break free. But

Cecile's grip tightened, and he couldn't escape, no matter how much he fought.

Her lips parted in a grin, her fangs shining red, and as he watched in horror, her grin continued to spread, until she was all grin and eyes. Joss opened his mouth to scream, but coughed instead. A searing pain ripped through his throat, and he realized that the blood that had pooled on the ground was coming from him. His free hand, now trembling, found his throat, which had been ripped open. As darkness overtook him, he thought the words that he could not speak. "Why, Cecile?"

He fell to the ground, and his sister's whispered words tickled his ear. "Because, Jossie. Because you killed me first."

· 12 ·

A QUESTION OF LOYALTY

Joss awoke in a cold sweat. He was bathing in guilt. But he couldn't determine if the dreams were really Cecile, reaching out from the grave to torment him with things he could not change, or his own immense, overpowering guilt at having taken a life and failing to preserve another.

Slipping out of bed, Joss rubbed his sore shoulder, but didn't dare touch his neck or his side. He was aching in the worst way, but also strangely relieved. Pain meant that he was still alive. And even more so, pain meant that last night had really happened, and Joss had really taken out the serial killer, like the Slayer

Society had charged him with doing. He was done now. He could go home. But first, he might try asking his uncle if there was any way they could spend a few extra weeks in New York. Like a vacation. A real vacation. Joss had never really been on one before.

He threw on some jeans and a T-shirt before moving painfully down the hall and down the stairs. When he entered the kitchen, all of the Slayers were waiting for him. He blinked at them, not certain what to make of the gathering, and moved his eyes from one Slayer to the next. Slowly, they began their applause. Then Abraham stepped forward and patted Joss roughly on the back. Joss winced at the pain this caused, but he wouldn't have traded it for the world. Abraham smiled. "Nephew, you were assigned a task and completed it in record time. I'm so proud of you. We're all proud of you. I've alerted the Society and they are thrilled. As a reward, you're finished working for the summer, and are free to enjoy a little vacation here in the city before returning home. Unless, of course, you'd prefer to go home now."

Joss could have floated, he was so happy. "I'd rather stay here for a bit longer, thanks. With you all."

His uncle patted his back once more, and though Joss winced at the pain again, he beamed. "Now, if you'll excuse me, nephew, I have some things to attend to in my study. But this afternoon, after all loose ends are neatly tied, perhaps you'll join me for some dinner? Just you and I?"

Joss grinned. "That would be awesome. Thank you."

He couldn't imagine spending time with his uncle where his every move wasn't being criticized. But it seemed that, with a single kill, an honorable takedown of a serial killing vampire, Joss had earned precisely that. He was almost dizzy with glee.

As Abraham excused himself upstairs, Paty beamed and set a large plate of breakfast on the table in front of Joss. The smells of bacon, eggs, and something sweet and bready filled his nostrils, and Joss nearly melted into a puddle right then and there. Smiling at Paty as he took a seat, he said, "So what exactly did he mean by 'loose ends'?"

Paty and Cratian exchanged knowing glances,

Joss took a seat, and Cratian offered him a semi-concerned glance as he shoved a huge forkful of eggs into his mouth. "Don't go crazy, stuffing yourself. We do have to visit the morgue after breakfast, and I'm betting you don't want to have too much in your stomach in case you lose any of it."

The fork stopped midshovel, and Joss's eyes shot straight to Cratian in shock. Morgue? They were going to the morgue? Why on earth would they go back there? There was no doubt at all about what had killed

Boris. Joss's stake had been the screwdriver, and Joss himself had caused the death. So why a trip to examine the body?

Paty waved Cratian's thoughts away as she filled a glass of orange juice and set it in front of Joss. "Oh, hush. Joss is tough. He can handle looking at a corpse and not barfing. I'm sure last time was just a fluke."

But Joss wasn't so sure. Seeing a corpse that had been sitting in a cooler for a few hours hadn't exactly helped his appetite. He returned his fork to the table. "I'm . . . not so hungry anymore, Paty. Sorry."

Paty frowned in disappointment. Cratian gave her a knowing smile. As quietly as he could, Joss excused himself and headed back upstairs. Suddenly, he had the urge to stand under a hot shower for a million years.

As Joss made his way down the hall, he settled on what he knew would be his only viable course of action before knocking softly on Abraham's bedroom door.

"Come in."

Joss turned the knob slowly, and stepped inside the room, sure to keep his footfalls light. Everyone else in the house was downstairs at breakfast, and he wanted to keep it that way. Just in case Uncle Abraham saw through his ruse and called him out on it. "Uncle Abraham, can I talk to you?"

Abraham was sitting in a chair in the corner of the room. Clutched in his hand was the book that Joss had seen him reading before. Judging by where Abraham's thumb was wedged between the pages, he'd all but finished reading whatever it was. His uncle was looking at him expectantly. Almost impatiently. Joss cleared his throat. "It's just that I can't shake this feeling . . ."

"Gut feeling?" Abraham set the book on the small table next to him.

"More like a nervous feeling." Joss resisted the urge to fidget. His uncle despised fidgeting, so he'd been working at holding his anxiousness inside. "Why are we going to the morgue to examine Boris's body?"

Abraham seemed to size him up for a moment before speaking again. In that moment, Joss felt like his entire face was on fire with guilt. Not that he had any reason to feel guilty. He had, in fact, according to his own uncle, done what no one had expected, and rid the city of a serial killing vampire. After a moment, Abraham leaned closer and said, "Whenever there is doubt in how a person or vampire died—"

"But—"

"—or doubt in a Slayer's loyalty, a body must be examined thoroughly."

Joss's stomach felt heavy, like a stone had been

dropped into his center. Straightening his shoulders, he said, "Oh. I see."

Abraham nodded. "It's not just you, Joss. Any Slayer who's under investigation has to be watched closely."

"I understand, Uncle." And Joss did understand. He just didn't like it very much at all.

His uncle reached for his book again, the mildest of concerns leaking into his tone. Joss knew that he cared. He might be a tough, mean gruff of a man, but in his own way, Abraham cared deeply about those who were important to him. Even, Joss knew, about him. "You'll be watched by Elysia now as well. You've taken down one of their own, and they won't forgive you for it. Are you sure you can handle it?"

"I'm sure." The lie escaped his lips so fast, he hadn't been completely certain that he'd spoken it aloud.

Abraham opened his book once again and waved Joss casually away. "All right then."

Joss still didn't feel very hungry.

· 13 ·

RETURN TO DEATH CITY

In comparison, Paty was much better at making
light of the fact that they were going to examine
a dead body than Morgan had been. Once they'd
entered the cooler room and slipped on their gloves,
Paty started humming a semi-happy tune. Then she
rubbed some kind of balm on her upper lip, to which
Joss raised a questioning eyebrow.

She held out the small container. "Want some? It
helps combat the stench. I honestly couldn't handle
being in here without it. That, and the humming.
Humming relaxes me."

After a brief pause, Joss dabbed his fingers in the container and smeared the contents on his upper lip. It smelled like mint with a hint of rosemary.

Unlike Morgan, Paty didn't even ask Joss to help in the examination. Not to touch anyway. But she did roll the body's left wrist over, so that Joss could see a strange tattoo. When he questioned its meaning, Paty said, "Vampires mark themselves with their name in the vampire language. We're not really sure why."

"And you can read it?"

Paty nodded. "Much of it, yes. About fifty years ago the Society learned quite a bit from a vampire who'd seemingly defected to our side. He taught us quite a bit of the language, how vampires hunt, what to look for in identifying them."

Joss mulled this over for a second. He wasn't certain why he was at all surprised that the beasts had no sense of loyalty. "Why didn't he teach you the entire language?"

"Because vampires killed him before he could." Paty clucked her tongue and shook her head. "A shame, really. He was quite useful to our cause. His efforts advanced the Society by leaps and bounds. Funny, isn't it? It took a vampire to teach us how to really kill vampires."

On the right biceps, Joss spied another grouping of

symbols, which looked similar to those on his wrist. Together, the symbols formed a square. "What's that, then? If this is his name . . . what is that?"

Paty bent down, turning her head this way and that. "It says something about brothers in arms. Something about four sides joined. I can't really read the rest."

Paty's cell phone rang and she put it to her ear. After a series of yeahs and mmhmms, she hung up and looked at Joss. "There's been another death. They think it's the same killer. This can't be our guy, Joss."

Joss cursed under his breath. He'd been so close. So close to being free of this task, and moving on to finding Cecile's murderer. He couldn't be wrong about Boris. He just couldn't. "Who found the body? Are they sure it's a vampire-caused death?"

As she returned her phone to her pocket, she said, "Morgan found it. And being that the head has been ripped clean off, and very little blood remained on the scene . . . yeah. It's a vampire. But you can judge for yourself in a few minutes."

Joss raised an eyebrow at her. "I can?"

"They're bringing the body here."

He gulped, and his heart picked up its pace. "Now?"

Paty offered a sympathetic smile. "What's the matter, kid? Nervous? You're already in a morgue with dead bodies. What difference will one more make?"

She was right, of course. It didn't make a difference at all, not really. But the idea of seeing yet another corpse—especially a headless one—was tilting his world on its side. Paty grabbed him by the shoulders, steadying him, and held his gaze, wordlessly asking if he was okay. Joss nodded and steadied himself on the cold metal gurney that held Boris's body.

The quiet keeper of the morgue opened the door to the cooler and barked, "Put it on the far gurney, the one that's missing a wheel."

He held the door open and Morgan backed into the room, carrying the broad end of a body bag. A moment later, Cratian entered, hefting the other end. They hoisted it onto the empty gurney with a sigh. Joss wondered exactly how much a dead body must weigh. He imagined it felt much heavier than a live one, but hoped he never had to find out.

But he wagered he would.

Cratian exited the room and returned with a small garbage bag. He dropped it on the gurney and met Joss's questioning eyes with a stern nod. "That's the head. Or rather, what was left of it. If you want anymore, go pick it off the sidewalk."

As Cratian stormed off, Paty looked at Morgan, "What's his problem? And why didn't the cleanup crew bring the body in?"

Morgan leaned with both hands on the broken

gurney. He sighed, letting his head hang for a while before answering. "This *is* the cleanup crew, Paty. Or rather, what's left of it. The others . . . we couldn't find enough pieces to even make out what was what or who was who. The Society said our cleanup crew failed to report after being called out to claim a suspected vampire victim in the Meatpacking District. They sent us out to investigate. This is what we found. It's a message. Loud and clear. The serial killer knows we're onto it, and it's not at all happy about it."

Joss swallowed hard. Their cleanup crew was dead. Not just dead. Obliterated. And whoever—whatever—had done it was coming for them next. How could he have been wrong about Boris? He'd been so sure. Unless . . .

He looked at the markings on Boris's biceps again. "You guys. What if Boris wasn't working alone? Everything he said, everything the vampire bartender told me about him said that he was our man, he was the killer. But what if he wasn't the *only* killer?"

The room grew silent as Paty tried to grasp what he was saying. Her breath came out in small clouds. Joss pointed at the tattoo. "What if he had brothers? I mean, what if the tattoo was a literal meaning, not a figurative one? Brothers in arms. It could mean that he and his brothers stick together, no matter what. And 'four sides joined'? Sounds like four brothers to me."

Realization lit up Paty's eyes, but overshadowing it was a dark cloud of concern. "If you're right . . . do you know what that means, Joss?"

Joss opened his mouth to tell her that yes, he did know. But before he could speak the words aloud, her voice echoed his thoughts into the cold room. "It means that our job—your job—just got four times more difficult."

He smiled a small smile—one that instantly drew a questioning glance from Paty. "No, it doesn't. It's only three times as hard. I've already killed one of them."

Paty chuckled and ruffled his hair. "Always the optimist, kid. You might just make it in the Society yet."

His chest felt warm and light, and only a little bit like his heart was glowing. "So what now?"

"Now . . ." Paty sighed. "You find Em. If she really is the oldest vampire in existence, she'll have something to say about a team of vampires running rampant. Just be careful."

Joss fought a yawn. It had already been a long day. The last thing he wanted was to seek out the world's oldest vampire when he was exhausted from killing her kind. But he had no choice.

Duty called.

· 14 ·

PERHAPS NOTHING AT ALL

Joss jerked awake on the subway train and sat up, wiping the drool from the corner of his mouth. He was surprised that the sudden movement hadn't sliced through his neck with pain, but then his bite seemed to be healing at a ridiculously fast rate. In fact, he doubted that there would be any remnants of it left by the next morning.

He hadn't meant to doze off, and if Uncle Abraham found out that Joss had fallen asleep—even for a moment—while on duty, he might just kill him. But Joss hadn't been sleeping well, and could see no time in the future when he'd rest well at all. A killer was still on the loose. Maybe several killers.

The nightmare he'd had this time—something to do with fire and blood—left him, but not as quickly as he hoped. One image, Cecile's mouth so large and strange and frightening, stuck with him the longest. Running a shaking hand over the back of his neck, Joss relaxed into his seat, cursing himself for having dozed off in public when killers were still on a rampage in the city.

"Everyone has bad dreams, Joss."

He jolted slightly at the sound of Dorian's voice. What was he doing here, in New York, and acting like Joss shouldn't be surprised to see him at all? Joss looked him over, not speaking for a moment, and wondered what the man who'd mysteriously brought his stake to him against the Society's wishes could possibly want from him. He felt on the defensive, until he looked into Dorian's eyes. Something about Dorian's expression told Joss that this man truly understood the torment that nightmares could bring. He cleared his throat, not wanting to talk about his dreams, and said, "I guess so."

Dorian didn't move, but instead sat very quietly, as if waiting for Joss to speak again. Joss shifted in his seat, wondering what Dorian was doing here, and how they just happened to end up sitting next to each other on the train. Dorian took a breath, let it out slowly, and said, "Like you, Joss, I frequently have terrible nightmares."

Every muscle in Joss's body tensed then. He had no idea how Dorian could know about Cecile. Did he? No. Of course not. Dorian couldn't peer into his soul, couldn't pierce his dreams and divulge the most private of details. But he had been sitting beside Joss as he'd dreamed. Maybe Joss had moved about. Maybe he'd talked in his sleep. It made sense. It also embarrassed him terribly. His nightmares were a secret—one between him and his dead sister. But then, he suspected, Dorian's nightmares were probably pretty secret, too, judging by his hushed tone, and the haunted look in his eyes. Joss relaxed his muscles some and leaned closer, dropping his voice to a conspiring whisper. "What do you dream about, Dorian?"

"I dream about a boy. He murders me every time I go to sleep." He sat very still for a moment, and when he moved at last, it was to wipe the smallest of tears from his right eye. "It's frightening, really. Because I don't know what the dreams mean exactly. And I'm not used to not knowing what my dreams mean."

The train came to a stop and the doors opened, letting an old man and a businesswoman on board. The old man shuffled by Joss and Dorian, but the woman stayed near the door, holding onto the bar above. Once the car began to move again, Joss turned back to Dorian. "Why do you think the dreams mean anything? I mean, dreams are just your subconscious going on vacation. Meaningless images flashing through your brain while you're asleep. They're just . . . dreams, right?"

At this, Dorian straightened, as if the subject of dreams were a passionate cause of his. "Dreams, my young friend, particularly to someone like me, and someone like you, believe it or not, mean absolutely everything."

Before the polite filter between his brain and his mouth could activate, Joss said, "Well, that sounds strangely ominous. What do you mean, exactly?"

As the train came to a stop, Dorian stood, his lips curled in a small smile. "We're just more alike than I think you realize, Joss."

Joss didn't like that. Didn't like the strange comparison between them when Dorian didn't really know him at all. He pursed his lips in anger. "How did you come to acquire my stake, Dorian? And why did you give it to me without the Society's permission?"

Dorian looked him over for a moment, like he'd been expecting Joss's anger. As he responded, he moved his eyes to the doors, answering without looking back at Joss. "I'll explain that soon enough. But first I think you should enjoy some of the nightlife my fair city has to offer. It would be far more advantageous to you than visiting V Bar. Especially considering the outrage you've created there. Might I suggest Element? Or perhaps The Vault? Both can be found in one building on East Houston and Essex Street."

As the doors swished open, people poured out onto the platform. In a blink, Dorian was gone.

Joss sat up in his seat, his eyes heavy with sleep. He looked around the car, but was surprised to find he had it all to himself. Had the entire conversation he'd just had been a dream? Had Dorian really been here, or were his restless nights finally catching up with him? His memory burned with the names of the nightclubs that Dorian had mentioned, but he didn't trust himself to recall them once he'd returned to base. So he withdrew a marker from his backpack and scribbled on his palm: *ELEMENT/THE VAULT—East Houston and Essex Street*. After a brief pause, he wrote: *Why would he suggest this?*

As Joss settled back into his seat, the buzz of curiosity filled him. Dorian had an intriguing way of popping into his world and back out again, of giving him things that he needed—like a stake, like a club name—and he never seemed to ask any questions. He simply knew things. Like how Joss had been experiencing a nightmare.

Joss wasn't an idiot. He realized that Dorian had some very vampirelike traits. But Dorian wasn't a vampire. Joss got the feeling that Dorian was something more. Something spectacular. He wasn't afraid of Dorian. And strangely, he almost trusted him. But he had to remind himself that vampires could do some strange, otherworldly things. Like control your thoughts, your actions, your memories, your feelings. They could create within you the desire for friendship, and only truth could rip that haze to shreds. Dorian was something other than human, certainly. But he was not Joss's friend.

As the train came to a stop, Joss stood, slipping the strap of his backpack over his right shoulder. He stepped off the car and navigated his way to the surface, slipping a pair of sunglasses on over his eyes to shade his vision from the afternoon glare. He moved down the street with a confident step, his peripheral vision always on the lookout for danger. The sounds of the city played out in his ears and Joss thought, not for the first time since he'd been here, that he could absolutely call Manhattan home. It was a busy place, a friendly place, with lots to see and do. The buildings were tall and interesting to look at, the people wearing kind smiles. In fact, if it weren't for the rampant vampire infestation, Joss was fairly certain he could be happy living in this city. But as they say, location is everything—and the last location a Slayer wants is living among the very vampires he's trying to extinguish.

Dorian had said that Joss had created outrage at V Bar. What was he talking about? Had Otis caused a ruckus over him being there? And, if so, what was he supposed to do, just give up his mission because his presence had ruffled some feathers? No. That would be cowardly. And Slayers didn't cower in fear in the face of danger. Slayers faced it head on.

It was this thought that carried him down the street and eventually, around the corner to V Bar. He hadn't been headed there at first. In fact, he'd been planning on checking out Obscura one more time and questioning the shopkeeper there. But something inside of him said to go back to V Bar, and that maybe he'd find Em there. As he turned the corner, he was met by a large crowd standing outside its blue doors. The sight of it made his steps slow, but after a moment, he moved forward again, into the crowd.

"Please, please, my brethren! If you'll all just calm down for a moment so that I may speak." The man standing on the steps of V Bar was the vampire who'd been with Otis the other day. The owner of the establishment. Enrico. Joss slipped behind a tall vampire in the back so that he could hear well enough without being seen. Only Enrico didn't speak. Not out loud, anyway.

Joss couldn't hear the vampire's telepathic words—not the way he'd been able to hear the bartender's thoughts before. And he wasn't entirely certain why he could hear one, but not the other. And he absolutely didn't want to ask any of his team members. What if it meant that something was wrong with him? He couldn't bear the idea of driving a wedge between himself and his Slayer family.

The crowd erupted in applause then, as if whatever it was that Enrico had thought to them had pleased them very much, and mutters raced through the group—mutters that spoke of vengeance and blood. Joss shrank inside himself. If they noticed him, he was as good as dead. "So please, ladies and gentlemen, allow your elders to handle this horrific situation. We promise to do so swiftly, and with the greatest of pleasures."

Dorian was right. Joss shouldn't have come here. He turned and slowly made his way back through the crowd. Just as he reached its edge, a hand fell on his arm, grasping it tightly. Joss gasped and turned his head to see Stephen, the bartender, gripping him like a madman.

Joss's heart beat harder, faster. All it would take was a word from Stephen and the crowd would devour him. Quite literally.

Stephen nodded slowly, and released him. "Did you keep your word, boy? Did he suffer?"

Joss dropped his gaze for a moment to the concrete beneath his feet. The concern and regret in the bartender's eyes was oddly touching, and Joss hated being moved by the mixture of emotions. Vampires weren't supposed to have emotions. They were monsters. Cruel, heartless, uncaring monsters. Weren't they? "I was as quick as I could be."

Stephen pinched the bridge of his nose, willing tears away, and then looked back at Joss. "Be quicker now. Get away from here. Don't return. They're out for your blood."

Joss nodded and moved away from the crowd. He didn't turn back to look at Boris's friend, but thought two words, hoping that Stephen would hear it. *"Thank you."*

By the time Joss reached the brownstone, his stomach was rumbling from a long day without much to eat. He'd made absolutely certain that he hadn't been followed back, but just in case he'd missed something, Joss passed their base of operations and paused at the corner, turning back casually to see if anyone unusual had paused as well. But no one on the street seemed even vaguely aware of him, or even mildly interested in where he might be headed. Satisfied, Joss hurried up the steps of the brownstone and stepped inside. Paty was standing guard in the foyer, looking bored as ever to be stuck with that detail. He flashed her a warm smile, but was met with a sad grimace. He liked Paty. She was like a tough older sister to him. "Hey, Paty. Slow day?"

Groaning, she sagged her shoulders a bit. "The slowest. But Morgan has door detail tomorrow, so at least I can get out of the house then. Turn anything up worth wondering about today, kid?"

Joss shrugged. "It's probably nothing, but I think I need to talk to my uncle about it. Where is he, anyway?"

"Out for the evening. Anything I can help with?"

Joss bit the inside of his cheek. He liked Paty, but she wasn't too keen on the idea of him taking risks. He needed someone who was. "Maybe. Where's Morgan, anyway?"

"In the library, looking at some old maps or something." Folding her arms in front of her chest, she tilted her head while looking at Joss, her tone lifting slightly in concern. "Everything okay, kiddo? You have big dark circles under your eyes, like you haven't been sleeping very well."

"I haven't. But I'm fine." He moved past her into the main hall then and made an immediate right, where he pushed open the double doors to the library.

Morgan was standing over the desk at the center of the room, poring over the large, haphazard pile of papers. He leaned on the desk with one palm, but his other hand was scratching furiously at his forehead. Joss cleared his throat and Morgan looked up at him, surprised. "Sorry, kid. Didn't hear you come in. What's up?"

Joss managed a shrug. "Long day."

Morgan sighed, his eyes scanning the papers on the table once again. "Tell me about it."

Joss nodded toward the papers. "What's all this about? More intel?"

Morgan sighed. "Kind of. Your uncle asked me to find more information on the vampires we're searching for. He says there has to be more to go on in our files, as everyone seems to be having trouble locating them. So of course I must have missed something. I had a friend in the Society archives fax several things over, and I've been linking that information all day with various articles and whatnot that I found online and printed out and . . . now I have a big, messy pile to contend with. Not to mention your uncle's complaints."

It was strangely nice to know that Joss wasn't the only one who felt pressure from Abraham. Still, Morgan's pursed lips and that deep crease in his forehead had Joss mildly concerned about what that stress might do to his health.

"I might have something." Joss felt the corner of his mouth twitch slightly. He had no idea how to tell Morgan that his latest lead had come from Dorian—and that Dorian might just be some kind of otherworldly creature. He wondered if Morgan would think him completely crazy if he told Morgan where his "something" was coming from. A dream? A vision? Something else altogether? He still had no idea. Maybe he was going crazy.

Morgan looked mildly hopeful. Or maybe he was just happy to have something other than a pile of papers to occupy his time. "What's that, little brother?"

Joss bit the inside of his cheek in hesitation before speaking. The little voice inside his brain begged him not to, but before it could start to make any more sense than it already did, Joss blurted out, "A lead. Maybe. I don't know, exactly. Do you know anything about Element, or a club called The Vault?"

A small crease formed on Morgan's forehead. He looked up briefly, as if perhaps the answers were in the ceiling tiles above. Not finding them there, he looked back at Joss and shrugged. "Maybe. Why?"

"Because I heard about it today, and I think we should check it out." *"Heard about it."* Not *"dreamed about it."* And certainly not *"hallucinated it."*

Morgan nodded. "Abraham will want a solid reason to investigate, y'know."

He was saying no already, before Joss had even had a chance to set foot inside the place to see whether or not Dorian's suggestion had been a dream or something else entirely. "My gut says we should do it anyway, Morgan."

After regarding Joss for a minute with a look that said he wanted to help, Morgan flipped through the papers sprawled across the desk. Near the bottom of the stack on the upper-left corner, Morgan produced a pink sheet of paper, covered with nearly unreadable handwritten notes. He slapped it down on top of the stack in front of Joss in a triumphant gesture, pointing to a paragraph on the center of the page that had the word "Element" scribbled across the top. "There. That place used to be owned by a vampire named Ignatius, but it changed ownership to a human about five years ago. Since then we've lost track."

"Why do you have this?"

Morgan looked exhausted, and very much like he was fighting a tired yawn. "I told you. Abraham wanted more information. So I went back a hundred years. Do you have any idea how much crap is in the New York files for the last hundred years? But this place caught my eye, so I kept it. Just in case it lead to something. Besides, it's got everything a vamp could want. Secluded areas, darkness. Whatcha thinkin', kid?"

Joss looked from the scribbled notes to Morgan and dared to say aloud his greatest hope. "I'm thinking we should hit the club tonight, Morgan. And I'm thinking there's no reason to tell my uncle about it until after we gather the information I think is waiting for us inside that club."

Morgan frowned, throwing a glance behind Joss at the door, likely checking to see if anyone were in the hall to overhear their little chat. Seemingly satisfied, he moved his eyes back to Joss. "Of course . . . while you could certainly pass as old enough to get into a club, your uncle would literally kill me for sneaking you into one, no matter what the reason."

Joss searched his mind for some excuse, some shred of semiconvincing reason that he could offer Morgan to get him to escort Joss into the club. But his mind came up blank.

Morgan snapped his fingers loudly, a grin on his face. "Got it!"

The enthusiasm in his voice caused Joss to raise an eyebrow in suspicion. "Got what?"

Morgan walked around the desk and gripped Joss's shoulders, a sparkle in his eyes. "Go get dressed. We're going clubbing, little brother."

· 15 ·

KAIGE

J oss walked alongside Morgan after they'd exited the subway station, nervously adjusting his red tie. It was hanging loose from his neck, the bottom tucked into his gray pinstriped vest, which was embroidered with bold black swirls that matched his black shirt. His pants were gray and black plaid, and topping off the ensemble were black Converse tennis shoes. Joss had argued with Paty over her fashion choices for the evening—after all, who wore Converse with a tie?—but in the end, he couldn't deny that he looked a little punk, pretty cool, and older than he actually was, which was certainly key to getting inside a nightclub when you had no legal business being there. As he walked, his shoulders straightened, and a small smile formed on his lips. For once, despite the fact that he was technically on the hunt for vampirekind, he was honestly feeling confident, and his smile was sincere.

Beside him, Morgan was dressed in short black leather boots, black pants, crisp black shirt unbuttoned at the neck, and a matching fedora. Morgan was smiling, too.

The tension that had infected the air between him and the other Slayers had melted away for the evening, and he and Morgan were just having a good time. For the first time, it felt like Joss had a big brother. Not a fellow Slayer. Not a mentor. Just a brother. One he could hang out with and just enjoy himself. They were going out on the town. They were heading out to a premier nightclub in New York City. The very idea of that, while slightly terrifying to a reserved fifteen-year-old, was immensely appealing.

A group of girls giggled past them and hurried across the street to a building that that looked a bit like an old bank. It was warmly lit, and outside was a line of people waiting to go in. Morgan paused at the corner. Joss paused beside him, squinting at Cratian's old driver's license. No one was stupid enough to believe that the fifteen-year-old guy holding the license was the twenty-one year old in the picture. They didn't look anything alike! Joss shook his head. "There's no way I'm getting in there."

Morgan sighed. "You are, too. You look older than you are, can carry yourself confidently, and the picture is kinda blurry. You wanted to know more about blending in in an urban environment? This is part of that."

"But Morgan . . ."

Morgan looked like he was losing his patience. "Look, kid. I have a contact at the door anyway, so getting into Element shouldn't be much of a problem. But getting downstairs, into The Vault, might be another issue. Let me do the talking, and if someone presses the issue of how old you are, just tell them you're a guest of Dorian."

Joss's heart seized in his chest. Morgan couldn't be talking about the same Dorian who had gifted Joss with a stake. Could he? He must have widened his eyes a bit, because Morgan looked at him and raised an eyebrow. "Everything okay, kid?"

"Yeah. Just . . ." Joss blinked, taking slow, deep breaths, trying to calm his heart rate. "Who's Dorian, anyway?"

A flash of suspicion crossed Morgan's eyes then. "The guy who owns the club, but not many know it. My buddy at the door said that if we so much as utter Dorian's name, it'll make people treat us right."

Joss nodded, his eyes on the nightclub across the street. He tried to appear calm but had a feeling his acting abilities were off tonight. The line at the door was growing.

In a moment, Morgan's hand was on his shoulder. "So exactly how do *you* know Dorian, little brother?"

The inside of Joss's chest felt like it burst into flames, flashing quickly with immense heat before turning to ashes and blowing away inside of him. He felt hollowed out. He felt empty. Slowly—so slowly that it seemed like time was barely clicking along at all—he turned his head and met Morgan's eyes. Morgan shrugged. "I could see it written on your face the moment I said his name. So how do you know him?"

The lie formed on Joss's tongue, but blew away like the ashes inside of him, leaving only truth behind. "He gave me my stake. My great-great-great-grandfather's stake."

Morgan eyed him momentarily before speaking. "I wondered where you got it."

Joss's eyes went wide. "You knew?"

Morgan nodded.

Joss felt his insides start to burn again. The heat permeated his flesh, warming his cheeks. "Do you know Dorian?"

Morgan shook his head, adjusting his fedora slightly with one hand. "No, kid. Never met the guy. And I'm highly suspicious as to why he'd give you a stake. But I knew somebody had, and I knew that it was through no doing of the Society. A tip, though: get a holster. You don't need to carry the case around in a bulky backpack. Most of that stuff, you'll hardly ever use."

A memory flashed through Joss's mind, the angry words of a vampire he'd once been friends with. Vlad had tossed Joss's container of holy water on the ground and given him a lesson that came out sounding like a warning. "Just so you know, the cross won't work either. They're myths—kinda like how all vampires are evil."

Joss chewed the inside of his cheek momentarily, mulling over the way that vampires kept managing to get close to him. He debated how Dorian kept seeping into his life, and wondered for a moment what this would mean for his future as a Slayer. With a hopeful tone, he muttered, "So . . . you're not going to tell my uncle that I carry a stake?"

"Tell him what? I'd rather you were armed." Morgan winked then and crossed the street. After a single heartbeat, Joss followed.

As they approached the line, Morgan led Joss right up to the front, much to the irritation of those who were already waiting in line. Morgan nodded to the doorman, who nodded back, ushering him and Joss inside.

It was a strange thing, walking into a club when you were very underage and clearly didn't belong. Joss had expected the crowd, the music, the line at the bar. But he hadn't expected a few of the leering glances from some of the women and some of the men. Morgan led him to the bar, where he grabbed a glass of some gold-looking liquid without ice, and Joss a glass of Mountain Dew with ice. They found an unoccupied bench and sat down, Morgan swirling his drink around in the glass before taking a healthy sip. Just as Joss was beginning to wonder what they were waiting for, Morgan leaned over and spoke as quietly as he could to be heard over the music. "See the guy at the bar? The one in the loose white shirt, tight leather pants, and snakeskin boots?"

Scanning the bar, Joss spotted the guy Morgan was talking about. His hair was long, semicurly, and dirty blond, his eyes such a crystalline blue that they could even be seen from this distance. And though he was obviously there alone, he seemed at complete ease with himself, as if frequenting clubs alone were a regular thing for him. It was, Joss assumed, largely because this man was a hunter, and nightclubs were clearly his hunting grounds. He wasn't a man at all—and Joss couldn't really identify his reasons for knowing this, beyond pure instinct—but a vampire. Joss casually moved his gaze away and sipped his Mountain Dew before replying to Morgan. "What about him?"

Morgan sipped his drink again, and Joss wondered if he were doing so to appear casual, or if he really needed a drink at that moment. "He's not alone. Look near the door."

Standing by the door was a woman, tall and lean. Her hair was black and sleek, hanging down to her waist. She was in a sparkly blue dress that fit her like it was two sizes too small, and heels so high that Joss wondered if they inhibited her movement at all. He hoped so, in fact, largely because Morgan was right. Two vampires were inside Element, and Joss wasn't exactly sure what he and Morgan were going to do about it. He sipped his Mountain Dew again, mulling over just that, and by the time he turned his attention back to Morgan, Morgan had stood and drained his glass dry. "Stay with him, kid. Watch him. Get close, but not too close. And if you need me, you call, okay? I'll come running."

Joss raised his eyebrows in surprise. "Where are you going?"

A smile settled on Morgan's lips as he nodded to the female vampire by the door. "With her."

Joss furrowed his brow, worried that perhaps she was using some kind of mind control on his friend.

"You do recall that she's a monster, right? And that we kill her kind? With good reason?"

As if Joss had slapped him, Morgan shot him a look. "If either of us has a chance of getting close to that thing and finding out what it knows, it's me."

He took this in for a moment, realizing quickly that he had insulted Morgan after Morgan had actually eased the tension between them for the time being. He was just worried, that's all. Worried that he couldn't trust Morgan's sensibilities, worried that yet another vampire would dupe him and he'd be left to pick up the shattered pieces of his existence once more. But, he reminded himself, Morgan was an old pro. Morgan knew how to tail vampires and how to get information from them without whipping out his stake and torturing it out of them. He looked at Morgan then and lowered his head a bit in shame. "Sorry, Morgan. I just—"

"I get the feeling you don't have many friends, little brother. But I want you to know that I *am* your friend. And I will never betray you. Not like Sirus. Okay?" Morgan held his gaze for a moment, letting his words sink in. They did. Deeply.

"Okay, Morgan."

"Hey . . . about that private job. If you ever want to talk about it—"

"I don't." Joss felt his jaw twitch slightly.

Morgan nodded slowly. "Too soon?"

"You could say that."

As Joss swallowed hard, Morgan cracked a sincere smile. "We're brothers, right?"

Joss nodded. They were brothers. Morgan was an important part of Joss's extended Slayer family. If he could trust anyone, he could trust a fellow Slayer. "Morgan?"

Morgan tilted his head curiously at Joss's inflection. "Yeah?"

"Holy water is useless against vampires, okay? Crosses, too. Just . . . just trust me on this, all right?"

Morgan seemed to mull this bit of information over for a moment. Joss could tell he desperately wanted to ask how Joss had come by this pertinent information, but in the end, he decided not to pry. He nodded slowly, and scratched his chin. "Good to know. Thanks, kid."

Joss wanted to tell him where that knowledge had come from—that it was from the mouth of a vampire he'd once called friend—but he couldn't. It was too embarrassing, having been duped twice by an undead creature of the night. He wanted Morgan to like him, respect him, admire him. How would Morgan ever do that if he knew that Joss was a Slayer who was incapable of recognizing his natural enemy? No. There was no way he could share the details of his encounter with Vlad with Morgan. Not now. Maybe not ever.

The female vampire turned and exited the door. Morgan tensed. "I have to tail her. You stay on him. Where he goes, you go. If you overhear anything about those vampire brothers, listen in, then hightail it back to base. You got it?"

But he didn't stick around for Joss's answer. Before Joss knew it, Morgan had slipped out into the night, leaving him alone in a nightclub in New York City. Unsettled, Joss took a drink of his soda and set the glass down on the small table to his right before turning his attention back to the vampire at the bar.

Except . . . the vampire wasn't there anymore.

Joss looked quickly around the club, but couldn't locate his mark anywhere. Frowning, he chastised himself for having lost the beast. But he wasn't about to go home empty-handed. The vampire hadn't gone out the door, so he had to be in here somewhere. Joss stood up, grabbed his glass, and headed for the stairs that led to The Vault. A large, meaty hand planted at the center of his chest, and the owner of that hand— who stood over a million feet tall and had shoulders the width of the Catskill Mountains—glared down at him with angry, slanted eyes. "Where you think you're going, son? In fact, how did you get in here in the first place?"

Joss swallowed hard, a small squeak preceding his reply. "Dorian. Dorian said I could be here."

The man didn't remove his hand, but with his free hand, withdrew his cell phone from his inside jacket pocket and flipped it open, pressing a button for a number on speed dial. His eyes stayed on Joss the entire time. "Yes, sir. It seems you have an underage guest in Element, trying to head down to The Vault. He says he's a friend of yours. His name is . . ."

Joss swallowed again. His throat was beginning to feel like someone had rubbed it over with a fine-grained sandpaper. When he spoke, his words came out in the form of a question, even though he hadn't intended them to. "Joss?"

The big man nodded. "He says his name is Joss, sir."

The pause between sentences must have only lasted a few seconds, but to Joss, they dragged on an eternity in length. And the entire time, his heart beat in slow motion. Loud, pounding beats thumping in his ears slowly. Solidly. When the man spoke again, Joss had to resist the urge to bolt. "I see."

Suddenly the meaty hand released Joss's chest, and the man's demeanor changed. He flicked his gaze around the room nervously. "I'm so sorry, sir. I didn't realize. Of course. Anything he wants, on the house. Yes. I apologize. I will. Right away, sir. Have a nice trip."

He closed the phone, returning it to his pocket then, and when he spoke to Joss, his voice was gentle and kind. "I'm so sorry, Mr. McMillan. I didn't realize you were in Dorian's inner circle. You have to understand my position. Young kid, nightclub full of . . . well . . . I'm so sorry. Anyway, whatever you want, sir. I'll get it for you. On the house, of course. Courtesy of Dorian."

Joss could feel his eyebrows threatening to go up in surprise, but he smiled politely and nodded, concealing his utter shock. "Thank you. No hard feelings. Hey, have you seen a blond guy in black leather pants and snakeskin boots around?"

An eager smile appeared on his face. "Do you mean Kaige? He just went downstairs. Do you want me to find him for you?"

Joss shook his head. The last thing he wanted was a vampire to be fully aware that a Slayer was looking for him. "No, I'll go look for him. Thanks anyway, though."

As he descended the stairs, Joss's entire being was enveloped by music with a heavy bass line. It thumped in his chest, down his legs, into the marrow of his bones. The lights were dim, as dim could be, and bodies filled every available inch of space. But something about the scene wasn't suffocating or intimidating at all. It was invigorating, energizing, and Joss liked the way that it felt.

As he moved through the crowd, people danced around him—some even tried to dance with him. Joss smiled politely and kept moving, his eyes sweeping the large space for any sign of Kaige. When he was just about to give up, he spotted the vampire in question talking to a girl in her midtwenties, who looked like she was falling over herself just to get closer to Kaige. Sometimes, Joss thought, he understood human girls as much as he understood vampires—meaning not at all.

He watched the vampire as casually as he could manage, and eventually, after an hour or so, Kaige grabbed the girl he'd been talking to by the wrist and tugged her toward the back of the club. The look on her face was one of blank obedience. She didn't seem intoxicated or anything, just like she was floating in some haze. A haze likely put there by a vampire. A cold shiver tickled its way up Joss's spine. He followed as discreetly as possible, darting between small groups of dancers, and eventually came to a door that was on its way to being closed. Pulling the door open, Joss peered up the dark stairs, running a hesitant hand over the back of his neck. Should he follow? He was just supposed to be gathering information. What if he was walking into some kind of trap?

Or worse. What if he didn't go up those stairs and an innocent girl was murdered because he didn't want to take a risk?

Joss stepped through the door and it swung closed behind him, sealing most of the music inside the club, leaving him with the faint sounds of bass still beating in his chest. As he moved up the stairs, he slid his back silently along the wall, traveling up several flights, doing what he could to remain in the shadows. At the top of the stairs was another door, and he placed his ear against it to listen. Nothing. Nothing but the sounds of the night. He took a deep breath, withdrew the stake from his waistband, and pushed the steel door open a crack.

He could only see a small portion of the roof from where he was standing, but he could see the vampire perfectly. Kaige was standing out on the roof, the unwitting, likely mind-controlled girl in his arms. He smiled down at her, his fangs shining in the low light. "Oh, my pretty little one. You should consider yourself special, my pet. It's not often in recent weeks that I feed in private. I like the thrill of killing you cattle in front of your own kind. It's rather addictive, that sensation. Every heart around me begins to race, filling my ears with a most delicious rhythm. It's the sweetest music I've ever heard. But I'm happy to forego that song tonight. Your AB negative has me salivating, and I don't want to share you. Not even with my brothers."

An emotion crossed his face then. Pain. Intense pain and loss. Kaige was grieving for his brother Boris.

But as quickly as that pain had surfaced, it disappeared again. "Not even in Central Park. Ohhh . . .

you'd like it there. Or, at least, I would. It's the only place where we hunt together, you see. I prefer to hunt as a pack, but Boris . . . well, he's always insisted that a hunt should be one on one. That it makes the moment more intimate. Of course, Boris is gone now. But I suspect you'd have enjoyed his company in Central Park. You could run free, until he pounced and drank your every drop. But not tonight. Tonight, you're mine, here and now. Shall we begin?"

Joss's stomach turned, then hardened with disgust. His fingers tightened around his stake and he pushed gently against the door, opening it farther. He had to get onto the roof, get as close as he could to the beast before it noticed him, and take it down. And standing here eavesdropping wasn't going to accomplish any of that.

Kaige paused momentarily, a smirk curling on his lips. "Of course, it would be very rude of us not to greet our guest, but then . . . he's being a bit rude too by lurking in the stairwell, isn't he?"

Joss grimaced and flung the door open. The steel hit the concrete wall with a loud bang. Kaige turned a surprised smile to him. Not surprised because of his presence, but perhaps because he'd been expecting someone else. "Well, well. The Slayers are recruiting younger and younger every year, aren't they? Must be getting desperate. Not that I can blame them."

Joss didn't say anything. Something his encounter with Vlad had taught him was that emotional distance from your mark makes it much easier to take their life. Hesitation is the most dangerous thing that can happen to a Slayer in confrontation, and interacting with the monsters might bring about empathy, which absolutely contributes to hesitancy. Besides that, Joss was human. That put him a few notches above vampire in his book. He'd save his conversation for someone who wasn't murdering innocents for sport.

When Joss didn't reply, Kaige said, "You've come to kill me, I assume? Mind if I finish my meal first? Even prisoners on death row are given a final meal."

His tone dripped with sarcasm, and it was all Joss could do to keep from losing his cool.

Joss scanned the roof, and apart from leaping off the edge, there didn't seem to be an easy manner of escape. Of course, if Boris had taught him anything, it was that vampires could fly.

Reaching to his left, he closed the steel door behind him, its metal sound clanging into the air again. He wasn't going to engage the beast. Talking wouldn't help the situation. With his hand gripping so tightly around his stake that his knuckles appeared bleached, he lowered his center of gravity, eyes locked on the vampire, ready to make his move.

Kaige shrugged and opened his mouth, lowering

it onto the girl's neck. But before he could bite, Joss broke into a run. In an instant, Kaige dropped the girl to the ground, ready for the Slayer's attack.

But Joss had other plans. He threw his stake as hard as he could, and it whipped through the air like a wooden missile, aimed straight for Kaige's heart.

At the last minute, Kaige pulled back. The stake struck him in the chest, but bounced uselessly off, its energy spent on its flight. Kaige grinned at Joss and moved toward him. Joss frowned at the ineffectiveness of his efforts, but noted that Kaige was moving only as fast as a human might move, which made him wonder if vampires each had different skills, and if maybe one of his was not speed. If his theory was true, then that would mean that vampires weren't insurmountable foes at all. It just meant that they each could do different things that he had to learn to work around. The thought comforted him some, but then Kaige was on him, ready for a fight.

He grabbed a handful of Joss's shirt, pulling Joss closer. And for a moment, Joss forgot that his opponent was supernatural at all. He balled up his fist and smashed it into Kaige's nose. Blood splattered across Kaige's face and Joss's fist in an explosion of anguished cries. When Kaige looked at Joss, his eyes were tearing, his fangs fully visible—but this time, not in hunger for the girl's blood.

Joss moved fast, grabbing Kaige by the wrist, hoping to surprise him. He flipped the vampire over, slamming him on the tar, scaring himself that he was even capable of such a physical act. Out of the corner of Joss's eye, he noticed a tattoo on Kaige's arm. It was the same tattoo that had been on Boris's arm: brothers in arms. Joss's theory had been correct. Boris had had a brother. Three of them, in fact. And Kaige was one of them.

The moment Kaige hit the ground on his back, Joss was on him, his stake in his hand, the tip pressed firmly against Kaige's chest. Joss looked at the girl, who had only just begun to stand back up again, completely dazed by what she had witnessed. "Go! Get out of here!"

The girl shook her head, but not in refusal. It was as if she were fighting to wake from a dream. She scrambled to her feet, her chest heaving in panic, and bolted for the door. After struggling with it for a moment, she pulled the door open and disappeared inside. Joss pressed the tip of his stake harder into Kaige's chest, until the skin broke and crimson bubbled up from within. He leaned closer to the monster's face, as close as he could without touching. "Now. Tell me where your brothers are."

Inside Joss's pocket, his cell phone buzzed to life. *Not now, Kat,* he thought. *Threaten my life later, but not now.*

Kaige's eyes were furious slits, but behind that fury lurked an emotion Joss was certain the creature hadn't experienced much of in its lifetime: fear. But outweighing that fear was its immense and utter hatred of Joss. It spit in Joss's face and growled, "Go to hell, Slayer boy."

"Bad boys go to hell. Especially when they send their sisters there."

Cecile's words echoed in Joss's brain then, just a fleeting, haunting whisper that Joss recognized instantly from a nightmare, but enough to loosen Joss's grip on his stake.

Spotting his opponent's moment of distracted weakness, Kaige threw a punch, smashing his fist into Joss's nose. Joss's head snapped back, pain exploding through his skull.

Then Kaige threw Joss off of him, sending Joss flying several yards across the rooftop. When Joss hit the tar, pain racked his body. Joss was certain he'd broken a bone or two or maybe all of them, but as he struggled the stand, only his muscles screamed out. And his nose, which hurt more than he ever thought it could.

Before he could fully recover, Kaige slammed into his side, knocking him into the wall. The wind left Joss's lungs, his chest seizing. For a moment, Joss had a feeling that these might be his last memories, that he might actually die on this roof.

Kaige gripped a handful of his hair and yanked his head to the side, hissing into his ear. "You've stolen my meal, Slayer boy. So now I'm afraid you're going to have to replace it."

Panic filled every cell in Joss's body. His heart raced until it was pounding in his ears. He pressed against Kaige, fighting to get free, but the vampire wasn't budging. Then Kaige laughed at his fear, breath tickling Joss's ear, and Joss's panic subsided. He'd trained for this, and panicking wasn't going to get him out of this situation. Then, in a moment of desperation, Joss had his target.

He lifted his knee as hard as he possibly could, slamming it into a place that no man wanted a knee slammed against. He had no idea if such a maneuver would even bother a vampire, but he had to try. And while Kaige didn't whimper or cry out or crumble to the ground, he did weaken his grasp enough for Joss to wriggle free. Maybe it had hurt. Or maybe he was just shocked that a Slayer had just kicked him in the balls in some stupid attempt to get free. It didn't matter to Joss. What mattered was that he had just evened the playing field a little bit more.

"For you, Cecile!" He whipped his arm forward

and the vampire caught it before he could make contact. Then Joss swung his other arm—the one holding the stake—with all his might. The silver tip plunged into Kaige's chest, and the wood in Joss's hand drove the weapon home. Blood—rich, red, real—poured out over his hand.

He pulled his arm back, freeing the stake. The sound that it made as the wood slid from the creature's chest tore through Joss's ears, causing him to cringe a bit. It was something he'd never forget. Blood continued to pour out over his hands, spilling onto the floor. Kaige's face was frozen in a state of shock. Joss looked from the open, gaping wound in Kaige's chest to his eyes. "Where are your brothers, Kaige? This has to end. Now."

Kaige coughed, sputtering some, a deep, gurgling sound escaping his lips. Joss pursed his lips, realizing he was too far gone to give any answers at all. Abraham would be furious.

As the light left Kaige's eyes and Kaige fell back, Joss watched him, a strange sadness cloaking Joss's entire being.

He'd taken a life. Granted, it had been the life of a monster, the life of a ruthless murderer. But it was still a life. A life that was no longer moving along in the world, having been blinked out by Joss and his wooden stake.

Sounds of the city at night echoed up around him, but all Joss could hear was the steady beating of his heart. It slowed a bit, calming, as he looked down at his prey. Inside he felt—no, that was the wrong word. He didn't feel. He simply was.

He stared down at Kaige's corpse for a while before crouching beside it, the bottoms of his sneakers turning red as blood pooled around them. He cleaned off his blood-covered stake and hands on a portion of Kaige's shirt that was still white and as he did, he looked back at Kaige's face. The brief, curious question of whether or not vampires believed in an afterlife flitted through his mind. Then he stood and slipped the stake into the back of his belt. He probably should have said something—to the corpse, to himself, to the midnight air—but in the end, he moved silently to the door. But before he could reach it, voices found their way up the stairwell. Voices that probably belonged to security guards, to police, to people in uniforms that had the power to make his life very difficult very quickly. Glancing around, Joss rushed to the edge of the building. There was no fire escape, no stairs. Just as he was beginning to consider the repercussions of jumping two stories, he spied a large pipe running from the roof all the way down to the street below.

With a deep breath, Joss flung his leg over the edge

of the building's lip and lowered himself onto the pipe, gripping it as tightly as he was able to. As he dropped from sight, the stairwell voices became the rooftop voices. He shimmied downward as fast as he could, slipping once, but regaining his balance fairly quickly. The moment his feet hit the concrete, he bolted into a run. Outside the club's front doors were four cop cars, lights flashing red and blue. Uniformed officers, guns in their hands, came out the door, their voices raised in command. Joss swore he heard one of them say something about a murderer. His chest ached as he ran. Was that what he was? A murderer? A killer? A criminal? When all he really wanted to be was a hero. All he really wanted to do was to help people, to save people from the monsters that stalked them. He'd read tons of comics growing up, where heroes like Batman and Spider-Man were looked down on as if they were criminals. Was this the same kind of thing? Was being a good guy or a bad guy merely a matter of point of view?

Was Joss Batman? Or was he the Joker, ready and hungry just to watch the world burn?

No, Joss thought as he ran down the street, coming to a stop a block away from Element. Joss was definitely Batman. The hero that the city, that humanity, didn't realize that they needed. But he was going to give it to them anyway.

Kaige was evil, and he was going to kill that girl. She might not recognize or remember that, but it was going to happen. And if Joss hadn't stepped in, she'd be dead by now. Yes, he'd taken a life. But it had come down to that girl's life and Kaige's, and luckily, the coin had fallen the right way. Joss refused to feel remorse. He'd done the right thing, and he'd argue that point home with anyone who wanted to question his actions.

Withdrawing his cell phone from his pocket, he pressed number two on speed dial and put the phone to his ear. "This is Joss. I need a cleanup on the rooftop of Element on East Houston at Essex. Police are on the scene. No pickup required."

The voice on the other end sounded monotone and unfeeling. "No cleanup crew available. Exit the scene until a replacement can be made available."

Cursing under his breath at having briefly forgotten about their eradicated cleanup crew, he hit END, marveling at how calm his voice had sounded, how in control, when he felt anything but.

Then he pressed number three on speed dial and waited for his uncle to answer. "I've got a lead, Uncle Abraham. Assemble everyone in the living room. I'll be home in a few minutes."

He turned back then, looking at the lights of the police cars from a distance as they flashed brightly against the surrounding buildings. People on the side-walk spoke animatedly and pointed at the building that held Element and The Vault. Police officers and security guards began a search around the perimeter of the building. Just as Joss was turning away from the scene, something gave him pause. It was the sight of a girl his age running up the front steps, into the night-club. She wore black and red striped tights, a black lace tutu, military combat boots, and what looked like a concert T-shirt from a band called The Mopey Teen-age Bears.

It was Em. Joss would have bet his stake that the girl he saw was the girl from his picture, the girl who wasn't a girl at all, but rather an inhuman, blood-drinking monster. From a distance, she looked a lot like Kat but Joss shook away that thought immedi-ately and turned from the scene, breaking into a run once again. He couldn't think about Kat right now, couldn't think about Sirus or last summer at all. He couldn't think about Em, or the fact that he was run-ning away, and leaving Morgan behind in the mix of so much chaos.

He could only think about getting back to base and washing the blood from his hands.

· 16 ·

IN THE COMPANY OF LIARS

A yawn escaped Joss as he climbed the brown-stone's front steps, but he shook it off. He was in no mood for another night's sleep, another evening of nightmares in which he would be tormented by a horrific version of his little sister. He knew he had the nightmares, but most times the details of which were extremely difficult to recall. Still, simply waking up with his heart racing, his body soaked with sweat, his tears drenching his cheeks was enough for him to want to keep the dream Cecile at bay. There were times, though he would never admit it to anyone else, when he wondered if the dream Cecile were actually real, rather than a part of his distorted subconscious. The idea scared the hell out of him, and made it even more difficult to fall asleep at night. Nightmare Cecile was terrifying, but he could deal with her. If she were actually real, actually his younger sister back from the dead and looking for revenge against her older brother . . . Joss might as well lock himself away in a padded room and hope that that was the worst of his life from here on out.

Uncle Abraham and the other Slayers were waiting in the living room, expectant expressions on their faces. Joss didn't sit, as it didn't seem like he was supposed to make himself cozy while he regaled the other Slayers with his tale of carnage. Cratian said, "So . . . Morgan has told us his side of the story. What's yours, exactly?"

Morgan stood at the other end of the room, looking down at the floor between his feet. Joss couldn't shake the feeling that they were in trouble, somehow. Even though this was what they were supposed to be doing. Killing vampires. Killing these vampires in particular.

Morgan shrugged, darting a glance at Joss with a hint of embarrassment. "I'm afraid mine got away from me, little brother."

Paty snorted. "Maybe it wouldn't have if you hadn't been so distracted by the short skirt."

The room grew very quiet, full of a tension that hung in the air, as thick as a New England fog.

Joss cleared his throat before beginning. Then he told them everything—everything but details of Dorian's involvement. Something in his gut told him that involving Dorian any more would create problems for him. Maybe for them both. Telling Morgan about Dorian was one thing. Telling Uncle Abraham would be quite another.

As he spoke, he kept his voice even and calm, answering the occasional question with ease. But one question—one asked by Ash—gave him pause. "How did you get into The Vault? From what I've heard, the bouncers there are pretty strict."

At this, even Morgan raised his eyebrows. Joss cleared his throat to buy some time—time in which he scrambled inside his mind for a reply that wouldn't implicate Dorian and his strange involvement in Joss's life. As he hurried to reply, not really knowing what he should say, the actor in him took the reins and smiled, cocking his head slightly to the side with sly confidence. "Let's just say I'm a smooth talker and leave it at that."

Cratian, Ash, Paty, and Morgan laughed aloud. Abraham did not. "And why exactly did you fail to follow protocol and keep the citizens of New York out of your mess?"

His smile crumbled, but no words came. But he suspected that that had been Abraham's intention. To silence him in the face of Joss's vanity.

Abraham stood as if to leave the room, and his movement stirred Joss's subconscious, bringing something important to the top. "There's one other thing."

"What's that?" his uncle inquired, an air of doubt hanging over his every word.

"I know where they prefer to hunt. And money says we'll find them there."

"Oh?" Abraham raised an eyebrow. "And where's that?"

Joss straightened his shoulders confidently. "Central Park."

Abraham grew quiet at first. Then he grunted. "We shall see."

The air carried a tension in it. Maybe it was because Joss had succeeded in killing Kaige, but everyone knew that there were more brothers out there to be dealt with.

Maybe it was nothing.

Later, as he dabbed hydrogen peroxide on the small cuts on his face and the few on his elbows and knees, Joss tried hard not to think too much about what had just transpired. He didn't think about the way that blood had sprayed from the vampire's body and splashed against his cheek. He merely watched the peroxide as it bubbled wildly against his wounds. On the surface, he was emotionless—a machine that served a single purpose and had dutifully fulfilled that purpose well tonight. The Slayer Society had tasked him with the destruction of a killer, of what had turned out to be a group of killers, and Joss had eradicated a second one.

Eradicated. It sounded so much more pleasant than killed.

The cut on his cheek was deeper than the rest, and Joss couldn't for the life of him recall the exact moment when he'd received that particular injury. He looked it over in the mirror, leaning closer to his reflection and tilting his head this way and that. There was no avoiding the fact that it needed to be stitched closed. If he forewent that nasty little task, he was going to have a scar. Joss might not have been as vain as many people viewed the McMillans, but the idea of a scar lining his cheek did bother him—even though his uncle Mike probably would elbow him and laugh and say that chicks dig scars. Joss wasn't at all girl crazy, but the idea of "chicks" digging him was pretty appealing. Still, he hated the idea of a scar on his face. So "chicks" would just have to find some other reason to dig him.

"What are you thinking about?" Paty was leaning against the doorjamb of the bathroom, overseeing his nursing skills. He was relieved that she'd followed him upstairs after his debriefing, and not one of the other Slayers. Paty was more gentle than the rest of his team, and what Joss really wanted right now was to be with someone who'd be gentle.

"Just wondering if what my uncle Mike told me is true. He said that chicks dig scars."

Paty grinned, her eyes on his wounded cheek. "Oh, yeah. You're going to have the ladies lining up around the block with that baby."

A laugh escaped Joss. It was pleasant and completely unexpected. Chasing it was curiosity. Maybe Paty, being a chick and all, knew what made chicks like someone. It was something to talk to Henry about, for sure.

Retrieving a large, sterile needle from a package inside the medicine cabinet, Joss reached for the bottle of rubbing alcohol and stitching thread. He'd seen Sirus sew stitches at the cabin last summer, and Sirus had kindly given him tips, just in case one day Joss would be sewing his own stitches. "The key," Sirus had said, "is to get your stitches as close together as you can. Keep them tight and you'll scar less. Take your time, focus on your task, and breathe through the pain."

Paty's forehead was lined with concern. "Are you sure you don't want me to do it? I'm fairly good with a needle. And it is on your pretty face, after all."

He shook his head. "I can do it."

"Listen. Joss. About what Abraham said at your debriefing . . ."

"It's okay, Paty." He'd snapped at her, and instantly regretted it. Flicking a glance her way, he nodded his apology. "It's really okay. He's right. I *was* messy. I should have taken Kaige down without the cops having been called."

Paty stepped forward then and placed her hands on his shoulders, meeting his eyes with warmth and understanding. "You did a great job. And I think you're right—I think we could find the other brothers in Central Park. Your uncle just struggles with the concept of encouragement, that's all. Don't worry. You're doing fine, Joss. Okay?"

It wasn't okay. But he knew that Paty wouldn't accept that as a reply, so instead he simply nodded again.

She glanced at the needle. "Want me to stay or go while you sew yourself up?"

He gestured to the door with his chin. "If you wouldn't mind. I'd rather do this part alone."

Just in case he cried. But he didn't say that part out loud.

Paty kissed his uncut cheek lightly and gave his shoulders a gentle squeeze before slipping out the door and closing it behind her.

Joss cleaned the already clean needle with alcohol,

as well as the thread and the wound itself. Then he threaded it, leaned close to his reflection, took a deep breath, and pinched his cut closed, shoving the needle through his skin.

The pain was burning and immediate, and before Joss realized that the voice was his, a string of curse words echoed into the room. But he pushed forward, looping the stitch as tightly as he possibly could, and poked the needle through again. By the fourth stitch, he hardly felt the pain—so grateful for endorphins that he almost thanked them aloud.

He finished up his sewing handiwork and tied a tiny knot at the end. After he washed the wound again, he looked closely at his stitching skills. It wasn't perfect, but it wasn't bad. The stitches were relatively close, and he was certain that Sirus would have given him a pat on the back if he were here.

But Sirus wasn't here. Sirus wasn't anywhere anymore. Sirus was dead. Because Joss had killed him. Like Joss had killed the vampire on the bar's roof tonight. And his brother in an alley the other night. Joss was a killer. A killer of vampires. It's what he did, who he was. And every time a vampire died, it brought him that much closer to soothing Cecile's tortured, restless soul.

Joss set his jaw and turned away from the mirror, unable, for the moment, to look himself in the eye.

· 17 ·

FAMILY DINNER

I t was late, but Joss was starving. He descended the stairs, only to find Ash and Cratian arguing over who got the last two pieces of bread in the house. Apparently, Joss's stomach wasn't the only one rumbling in the late night.

Paty stood, clapping her hands together, as if to punctuate the end of their argument. "I'm starving. Who's up for a late night dinner out?"

Abraham said, "I know a wonderful restaurant not far from here."

Morgan raised an eyebrow, clearly suspicious. "You buying, boss?"

Without replying, Abraham stood and exited the room. Joss exchanged glances with the other Slayers, but no one further questioned Abraham's sudden onset of generosity. They merely stood and made their way to the door. As they filed out the front door, Abraham placed a hand on Joss's shoulder, stopping him briefly. Then he called to the others, "Two blocks east. You can't miss it. Has striped awnings. We'll be along shortly."

He watched the other Slayers move forward for a moment before speaking to his nephew in a low, somber voice. "Don't think me a fool, boy. I'm well aware that both you and Morgan are keeping something from us. And if you think I won't find out the details of your little secret, you are sorely mistaken."

Joss swallowed, his throat burning for a moment. The heat quickly found its way up and out, setting his skin aflame with guilt. He opened his mouth to say something—anything, really, that might set his uncle's suspicions at ease—but then closed it again. Nothing he could say would make his uncle believe him. Not even if he had nothing to hide.

But he did have something to hide. And for some reason, Morgan seemed to think that hiding the fact that Joss knew Dorian was a good idea. So Joss followed suit and gave away no secrets.

Instead, he looked his uncle in the eye and said,

"Uncle, I have no idea what you're insinuating, but Morgan and I have nothing to hide. And quite frankly, your tone seems a bit edged in panic and conspiracy."

The corner of Abraham's mouth lifted in a strange smile then and he turned away. For a moment, Joss thought that their conversation was over and that Abraham was leaving without further comment. But then his uncle turned back to him and gripped the front of his shirt with his hand, twisting the fabric until Joss was convinced that it would rip. To his surprise, the fabric held. Abraham pulled him closer and as he spoke, his words didn't seem like words at all, but a bit like steam after water has been dripped onto a hot surface. "Don't think you can pull one over on me, boy. I've seen things, done things that would curl the hair on your backside. I've lived ten lifetimes with one life, and I can spot a liar a hundred yards away."

Joss's heart betrayed him, picking up its pace with a steady *thump-thump-thump*. As his uncle pulled him even closer, until their noses were almost touching, his heart almost stopped.

Abraham hissed, "And you, boy, are a liar."

The actor Joss set his jaw and then forced a calm smile. "Think what you want about me, old man."

When Abraham released him, he did so forcefully, shoving Joss backward, as if he couldn't stand to be in his company for even a moment longer. Joss stumbled, but regained his composure, and then smoothed out the wrinkles in the front of his shirt. Without another glance at his uncle, he turned and walked in the direction that the other Slayers had. He found them two blocks up. Morgan immediately leaned over and quietly said, "Everything okay, little brother?"

He nodded in response, wondering if Morgan could read the anger in his eyes. Something told him that Morgan could see through the actor to the real Joss within. "Fine. Everything's fine. But I'm a liar and he knows it."

Morgan nodded. "I'm a liar, too, kid. But so are poker players. And a good cardshark knows when to show their hand, and when to keep their mouth shut."

Joss regarded him for a moment as he listened to his uncle's steps approaching softly behind him. He had the distinct impression that Morgan was not only telling him that it was okay that they'd lied to his uncle. He was also saying that they should keep lying to him. Until . . .

Well. Joss had no idea until when. But he did know one thing. He trusted Morgan.

The tiny hairs on the back of his neck. He'd trusted Sirus, too. And at one point in time, he'd trusted Vlad. What did that say about his level of trust in people? Maybe he was incapable of trusting the right people.

Maybe Morgan was someone that he shouldn't be listening to at all.

From the outside, the restaurant looked like any other small Manhattan eatery. And from the inside, it was much the same. So Joss couldn't figure out exactly why his uncle's energy seemed to suggest that this was absolutely the place to dine in New York City. Regardless, Abraham strode inside and approached the hostess with the air of someone who was greatly pleased with himself. "There are six of us tonight, dear. Would it be too much trouble to locate a private table in the room? Something with atmosphere?"

The hostess smiled and scanned the pile of papers on her podium for a moment before answering. "Yes. I think that's something we can arrange, sir."

Then Abraham leaned closer to her, a whisper escaping his lips—words that Joss could not distinguish, no matter how hard he strained his hearing. When he was finished, the hostess smiled brightly and said, "Certainly, sir. Now if you'll all please follow me."

She led them through the dimly lit room to a large round table in the far corner. Once they were all seated, a man stepped forward and smiled. "Good evening, everyone. My name is Markus. I'll be serving you tonight. Can I get everyone's drink order?"

But before Joss could utter the words *Mountain*

Dew, the hostess whispered to Markus, who smiled and said, "Of course! Right away."

Markus—who Joss highly suspected of simply being Mark when he wasn't working at a hip, posh restaurant—disappeared and a moment later was replaced by a lean man with long black hair that curled at the ends. His eyes were bright green, and when he smiled, Joss felt a strange wave of caution move through his insides. When he approached the table, he stood behind Morgan's chair and said, "Good evening, all. I'm Jacques, the owner of this establishment. Markus tells me that my company has been requested at your table. Is everything to your liking so far?"

As Joss watched, the color bled from Morgan's face, and everything that made Morgan . . . well, Morgan . . . went away in a flush of shock. He turned around slowly, and when he and the owner locked eyes, the air left the room. Abraham sat back in his chair and smiled.

Jacques glanced at each of Morgan's tablemates before clapping his hands together—hands that might have been trembling in surprise, Joss didn't know. "Champagne. The best we have. Excuse me. I won't be a moment."

Once he'd left the table, some of the color returned to Morgan's face, but not much. Joss leaned over to him and said, "Do you two know each other?"

Morgan sipped his water, but pursed his lips, as if it tasted bitter. Something about the look on his face said that it had nothing to do with the water. "I wouldn't say that."

Joss furrowed his brow, confused. "It . . . just looked like you'd spoken before."

Morgan raised his glass then, and Joss had a feeling he wished that it were something a bit stronger than water. He set the glass down, a bit harder than was necessary. And when he turned his eyes to Joss, Joss could see the threat of furious tears lurking in Morgan's baby blues. "Once upon a time, that man was my brother."

Joss looked over at the man at the bar. He could certainly see a resemblance. But Morgan's use of past tense only confounded him further. "He's not anymore? What happened?"

Morgan followed Joss's eyes to the man in question. Under his breath, he said, "He died."

· 18 ·

BLOOD BROTHERS

J oss chewed each bite of steak carefully, and when
Jacques asked if anyone wanted dessert, he ordered a slice of cheesecake, but truth be told, he
wasn't feeling very hungry. From across the room,
he watched Morgan's brother, who watched Morgan,
who tried to act as if he wasn't even aware that his
dead brother was standing in the same restaurant as
he. Dinner conversation was awkward, and glances
across the table, full of concern and questioning, made
it even more awkward. The only one who seemed
completely at ease was Abraham, who had just wolfed
down a big fillet and was looking forward to dessert

like nobody's business. Joss kept an eye on Morgan's rocks glass, but it had been emptied a few times now, and he was pretty sure it wasn't helping him feel any better about what was bothering him.

Morgan stared forward, eyes glazed, and when Jacques asked what he'd like for dessert, Morgan growled, "A double."

Dessert came and so did Morgan's drink, and all Joss could think about was getting out of this place, and getting Morgan away from the specter across the room. Jacques had no sooner set a new glass on the table than Morgan gripped the glass and lifted it to his mouth, emptying a third of it in a single swig.

Joss exchanged glances with Paty, who seemed just as confounded as he felt. Morgan immediately lifted the glass to his lips again and practically inhaled a mouthful. Paty's jaw hit the floor. "Wow, Morgan. Need a drink much? A few drinks? What's that, your third double?"

Morgan didn't even glance her way before taking another swig. Something told Joss that it would be wise for him to keep his mouth shut, so he did just that.

An enormous slice of cheesecake came on a plate painted with lovely images, created from strawberry glaze and berries, but Joss set it to the side, unable to eat even another bite. After devouring his dessert in two satisfied bites, Abraham sat back in his seat, carefully wiping his mouth clean with his napkin and setting it on the table before turning his eyes to Joss. There was an air about him that suggested that, for his uncle, anyway, the real dessert was about to begin. "Did you enjoy your meal, nephew?"

Joss looked up, ripped from his thoughts. He looked at his plate, still full of uneaten food, and set his fork down beside it. "Absolutely. It was delicious. I'm just . . . not very hungry."

Of course he wasn't hungry. It was hard to eat with waves of immense hurt and fury coming off Morgan like this.

Abraham turned his eyes, setting his sights on the subject of Joss's distracted thoughts. His words sounded like they'd been given through smirked lips, but Abraham's expression held no such thing. "How did you like the service tonight, Morgan?"

He drained his glass of amber liquid, leaving behind a few lonely ice cubes that rattled as Morgan slammed it on the table in front of him. When he looked at Abraham, his expression made Joss cringe. Everyone else at the table grew eerily silent. Morgan's words seeped out of him in a hiss. "You have a sick sense of humor, Abraham."

Abraham seemed completely unaffected. "And you have a flawed sense of loyalty."

Morgan dropped his eyes to his now empty glass. It looked very much like he wished it were full again. "Meaning what, exactly?"

"You know very well what I mean." Abraham sat forward in his seat, eyes on Morgan the entire time. "How did you get into that club? What exactly is it that you're hiding from us?"

Joss's heart picked up its pace. There was no way his uncle was going to let this go, let it slide away into the land of the forgotten. This battle of wills was apparently too important to him to lose.

Morgan picked up his glass again and lifted it to his lips, as if he could coax more of the amber liquid to appear. When he set his glass back on the table—quieter this time—his voice was softer. "I am hiding nothing at all from the group, Abraham. And it sickens me that you would go to these lengths to try to uncover some fictional conspiracy that you've cooked up in your mind."

"To what lengths are you referring, exactly?" Abraham shook his head, toying with him. "Come, come. No secrets among friends and Slayers. Am I right?"

Morgan's jaw was so visibly tight that Joss was quite concerned that he might grind his teeth down to nothing, if he wasn't careful. "You knew that Jack—or Jacques, as he's calling himself now—was my brother. Before he . . . turned."

Abraham nodded. "By choice. Your brother chose to become a vampire. True?"

Morgan looked around the table, at each face but Abraham's, before offering up a response. When he spoke, a cloak of shame seemed to fall over his features. "It's true. Jack came to me ten years ago, when I was fifteen, and told me that he'd arranged to become a vampire. He wanted my blessing, but I refused. Until tonight, we hadn't spoken since that day. I vowed never to see him again."

Joss glanced at his fellow Slayers. Each of them darted a questioning look at Abraham, who folded his arms in front of him. "Don't make this about pity, Morgan. I brought you here tonight to remind you that I'm well aware of your dishonest nature. When your father and I approached you at the age of eighteen and informed you that you were a Slayer, we asked if you knew anything at all about Jack's strange disappearance three years prior. You shook your head and said that you had no idea what had happened to him. A lie, correct?"

Morgan hung his head in response.

Abraham nodded, as if answering for Morgan. All eyes were on him. "Yes. It was a lie. Because until you turned twenty-one, you and Jack were still in contact, albeit secretly. Even tonight you lie, stating that you'd never spoken to him after the night he confessed to you when in all actuality, you were quite close for several years after he turned. Correct?"

Morgan had slumped in his seat. Joss couldn't decide if he looked broken or relieved. "I kept his secret. He was my brother. What was I supposed to do?"

"You were supposed to tell the Society." As the words escaped Joss, they surprised even him. They weren't full of accusation or superiority. He wasn't judging Morgan in the slightest manner. His words were simply a matter of fact. In a situation like that, no matter how deep you are into the web of lies you've created, a Slayer is expected to confess all to the Slayer Society. And in a way, doing so unburdens the Slayer.

Joss swallowed hard and looked at his uncle. The sudden, jolting urge to tell him all about Dorian seized Joss. Looking over at Morgan, the urge didn't dissipate at all. Did he really want to be in the state that Morgan was in a few years? Did he seriously plan to keep this secret hidden, when he had no proof that keeping it would help him in any way?

Abraham met his eyes and the word *no* rang through Joss's thoughts, loud and clear.

"Something you care to add, Joss?"

For a moment, Joss allowed his lips to part. He let the confession form on his tongue, where it sat like a bitter pill before he swallowed it down, its jagged edges scraping against his throat. He couldn't escape the feeling that telling Abraham about Dorian would be a huge mistake even though he had no reason to think so. And he really disliked the way that Abraham was trying to bully a confession out of Morgan by involving the brother that Morgan had, for some reason, cut out of his life. So with the bitter confession trailing its way down his throat, leaving behind a nasty aftertaste that reminded Joss of old pennies, he looked his uncle dead in the eye and said, "What do you suppose the Society would think of what you're doing to Morgan right now? Do you think they'd approve, be proud?"

He didn't mention the fact that the Slayer Society would likely want Morgan to kill his brother, Jacques, and hoped that Abraham wouldn't either. "I don't. I think they'd be pretty disgusted with the way you're handling this. Neither Morgan nor I are keeping any secrets from the Society, Uncle. I suggest you make peace with that."

Abraham raised an eyebrow. "Or?"

Joss plucked a cherry from his glass and popped into his mouth. "Or I'll report you for needlessly harassing your fellow Slayers."

At this, the table grew extremely silent. It was a serious charge, and unless Abraham could somehow uncover their secret to support his defense, it was highly unlikely that he'd escape that charge punishment free. Abraham's shoulders visibly tensed, though it was clear by the look on his face that the last thing he wanted was for his nephew to comprehend that he was feeling even slightly on edge at the notion of being formally charged by a fellow Slayer. Especially a fledgling Slayer like his nephew. He looked at the table for a moment before returning his gaze to his nephew. "All right. I can see how this is going. So I'll ask once more and then drop it forever, Joss. Is there or is there not something that you and Morgan are keeping from me?"

Joss tensed his jaw in irritation at Abraham's persistence. "Uncle, if either of us had anything at all to tell you, I assure you that we would."

Joss wasn't sure why he felt the need to keep Dorian a secret, or why Morgan felt the need to protect Joss's secret. He just couldn't bring up anything about Dorian. Not yet. Not until he'd learned why Dorian had given him his stake.

Abraham watched him for a while before nodding. Whether it was in agreement or a way of saying that he knew the truth lurking in Joss's expression, Joss had no idea. He only knew that the matter was settled for the moment, and they could return to base without continuing the argument.

Abraham dropped cash on the table, and as the group made their way to the door, Joss couldn't help but notice the distinct lack of Morgan's presence. He looked back and found Morgan in a heated conversation with his brother at the table they'd just left. His brother reached out to grab him by the sleeve, but Morgan violently shook his sibling off and growled, "No, Jack! What part of *never* don't you understand?"

Morgan pulled away from him and brushed roughly past Joss. As he did so, Jack—the once-man who was the now-vampire Jacques—called after him, his voice full of heartbreak, "You came to me, Morgan! Remember that!"

Then Jacques met Joss's eyes. "Please. Watch after him."

"Morgan can watch after himself." Joss set his jaw. He couldn't believe that this was Morgan's brother, despite the facial similarities.

Jacques shook his head. "Not now. Not with all of Elysia out for your heads."

Joss looked at him, at this man who had been Morgan's closest relative at one point in time. "Then help us end our stay here, Jacques. Do you know where the remaining brothers are?"

Jacques grew quiet, his eyes flicking around the room momentarily. He whispered, "I cannot tell you. They would have my head. But . . . you're right, young one. They are like animals."

Without another word, Joss nodded and moved out the door, joining his fellow Slayers half a block up. He walked in step beside Morgan, neither of them speaking, until the rest of the Slayers had filed into their base of operations in front of them. As soon as they did, Morgan stopped Joss with a hand on his shoulder. His eyes were red and moist, as if the tears that he'd been holding in were finding their way out against his will. "Joss," he said, his voice shaking slightly, "thanks for sticking up for me. Your uncle . . . he can be difficult, y'know? Of course you know. If anyone knows, you do."

Joss nodded in response. He did know. Abraham wasn't exactly the easiest person on the planet to get along with. It wasn't like Joss disliked him. In fact, he greatly admired his uncle. But Abraham's affections were not easily won. Not by a long shot. "No problem, Morgan. But hey . . . about your brother . . . you okay?"

Morgan shook his head. "Whether I am or not is none of your concern, little brother. Don't give it a second thought. Not even about your uncle. I don't hold grudges and won't start now, so it's best we just leave my past in the dark where it belongs."

A hot pain passed through Joss's center. "Morgan . . . you're not the only person to have lost someone because of vampires, y'know."

Morgan nodded. He knew about Cecile. Of course he did. They all probably did. The idea of them all knowing his darkest secret made Joss's stomach flip-flop.

"You're right, little brother. But knowing that doesn't make it any easier to face having lost them. Am I right?"

His stomach still doing a flip-flop, Joss nodded in agreement. Just as nothing that Morgan could say to him or share with him could ever ease the pain of losing Cecile, nothing at all that Joss could say or do could possibly make Morgan feel any better over losing his brother to the vampires. After a moment of shared silence, Morgan climbed the steps to the brownstone and soon after, Joss followed.

As he passed the open library doors, Abraham called to him. "Oh, Joss. I was meaning to ask you over dinner. How do you propose we should proceed in our continued search for the two remaining vampire brothers? In other words, when are we taking a little field trip to Central Park, exactly?"

Joss bristled. "Tomorrow night, Uncle."

Abraham raised his eyebrows slightly, as if he were mildly impressed. "Tomorrow night, nephew. Alert the team, if you would, over breakfast. Except for Morgan, who won't be joining us."

Joss furrowed his brow in concern. "Why won't he?"

Abraham plucked a newspaper from the table next to the chair he sat in and smoothed it out in front of him. "Because. I'm not sure I can trust him on my team, or with my nephew. His brother, it turns out, is quite close to a vampire who tried to kill me twice now. And I fear that Morgan may be feeding him information."

"Uncle Abraham, Morgan is—"

"Have you learned nothing from that whole experience with Sirus last summer, Joss?"

Abraham's words were so jarring that they hit Joss in the center of the chest like a fist. He stammered to speak. "Of . . . of course I have."

Abraham looked him over before turning his eyes to an article in the paper. "Good. Then alert the team over breakfast. Sans Morgan."

Joss's chest still ached from his uncle's jab. One thing was for certain about Abraham McMillan. He pulled no punches. If your baby was ugly, he was going to tell you all about it. "And if Morgan asks why he's not invited? What should I say?"

Abraham's eyes were scanning the words on the page, as if he'd already completed his half of the conversation they were having. "He won't. He'll already know."

Joss didn't want to question how Abraham knew this, but he suspected it was because he and Abraham had worked together for so long. Abraham knew

Morgan better than Joss did. So if he said that Morgan would react in a certain way, then Joss was inclined to trust him.

He nodded at his uncle and turned to leave the library. As he moved up the stairs, Joss's footsteps felt heavy, growing heavier with every step he took. He didn't much care for the fact that he had to tell everyone that they'd be doing a stakeout in Central Park, and he cared less that he'd have to be the one to tell Morgan that he wasn't coming along. He liked Morgan. Despite the fact that Morgan's brother was a vamp. And despite the weird sensation that maybe he couldn't trust Morgan, couldn't trust anyone.

As he entered his room to get ready for bed, Joss had a terrifying thought.

What if he would never be able to trust anyone ever again?

It lingered in the forefront of his mind as he stripped down to his boxers. As he brushed his teeth. As he climbed into bed. As he pulled the sheet up to his waist. And when he closed his eyes and slipped off to sleep, his nightmares were not about Cecile, but about the immense, immeasurable length of his life that he might spend irrevocably and utterly alone.

· 19 ·

AN EVENING IN CENTRAL PARK

The next morning, Joss took his time showering and going through his morning routine. When he opened the bathroom door, Paty passed by, a mug of coffee clutched in her right hand. She grunted a *g'mornin'* in his direction, and Joss stepped out into the hall. The smell of bacon filled the air, beckoning to him from the kitchen downstairs. Behind him, he heard footsteps.

He turned to see Morgan coming down the hall. Morgan nodded to him, but said nothing. As he passed, Joss almost said something—hello, good morning, something—but then, for whatever reason, he didn't.

Instead he followed Morgan down the stairs and into the kitchen, joining the others at the table, which was filled with plates heaping with bacon, scrambled eggs, and toast. The smells were so good that Joss wondered if the way the food tasted could possibly live up to it. He bit into a slice of buttered toast as Paty heaped a small mountain of scrambled eggs onto his plate, and its crunchy texture melted onto his tongue. An *mmmm* sound escaped him before he realized it was he who made it. Ash and Paty chuckled before Paty said, "Hungry much, kid?"

Joss belched, which erupted more laughter.

After they'd eaten most of what was on the table, and it had become crystal clear that Abraham wouldn't be joining them, Joss set his fork down, wiped his mouth with his napkin, sipped his orange juice, and said, "So I have a plan."

Ash, Cratian, Paty, and Morgan looked his way, their eyes full of curiosity, and Morgan's tinged with sadness. In the most determined tone possible, Joss said, "Tonight we're staking out Central Park. I overheard Kaige telling his intended victim about hunting there, so the smart thing to do is to investigate the area, and see if maybe we can locate the remaining two brothers. I've killed two. That means there are just two left before we're done with this job. So let's get out there and stake these things, so we can all sleep a little better at night."

To his surprise—maybe he'd expected more laughter or a few shaking heads—all three Slayers nodded slowly, admiration sparkling in their eyes. Morgan reached over and gave his back a pat. "Sounds like a solid plan, little brother. You plan on stopping by the morgue first, right? To inspect Kaige's body?"

"Of course." Joss smiled, biting the inside of his cheek, bracing himself for his next words. He met Morgan's eyes and took a slow breath. "Oh, and there's just one thing. Morgan, you won't be joining us."

Morgan nodded just as slowly as Joss had breathed. "Of course not. I'm compromised, because of my brother. It's all right. I need to spend a little time organizing my notes on what we know about Elysia in New York anyway."

At that moment, Joss realized something that shook him a bit. His inner actor was clearly superior to Morgan's, because at the moment, despite his reassuring smile, Morgan's actor was failing completely at passing off his disappointment for casual tones.

They cleared the table quietly, and as Cratian was placing the last plate inside the dishwasher, he turned back to Joss, who was wiping down the counters with a sponge. "What time are we staking out the park, kid?"

Joss pulled a time out of the air, hoping it sounded like a wise idea. "Nine o'clock. We'll assemble in the library about a half hour before."

"Don't worry about Kaige. I'll inspect his corpse. Compromised or not, I'm good enough to pick at a dead body, if nothing else. You guys worry about the task at hand." Morgan's words lacked emotion, as did the expression on his face. His inner actor, apparently, had found the strength for Act Two. He finished folding the kitchen towel and hung it over the oven door bar. Then he quietly left the room, leaving the others exchanging glances full of pity. But there was no changing it. Abraham had given explicit instruction that Morgan was not to join their stakeout, so Joss had no choice but to listen.

Joss spent most of the day writing in the journal in the back of his field guide, annotating everything he'd experienced over the last few days. When he finished, he read over some of the notes that Morgan had given him regarding the vampire brothers and what the Society knew about them, which wasn't much. Then, whether in preparation for a late-night stakeout or completely by accident, Joss fell asleep.

He, thankfully, did not dream.

He awoke just past eight that evening, and made his way down to the kitchen to make himself a sandwich for dinner. Then, glancing at the clock, he gathered his Slayer tools and moved into the library to wait for his team. He was joined shortly by Ash and Paty, followed soon by Cratian and his uncle Abraham. In a few minutes, they'd assembled and moved out the front door, leaving Morgan behind to deal with Kaige's remains.

If someone had covered Joss's eyes and ears and led him to the heart of Central Park before allowing him to see and hear where he was, he would never have guessed that he was in the middle of the largest, most populated city in the United States. All around him were trees and greenery, wildlife, and the quiet sounds of nature. He couldn't help but marvel that a place that offered such serenity existed in such an exciting metropolis, and yet here it was, covering more ground than he had ever dared imagine. It was beautiful. The cityscape was beautiful, too, but this . . . this was different.

Paty looked less than impressed as she stepped up beside Joss. Her lips were pursed, her eyes glazed from the immediate onset of boredom. When she sighed, Joss knew that it was for him—a reminder, perhaps, that he was the one who'd brought them here, and if nothing turned up from this little field trip, that it would be his fault that she'd wasted a night in the woods, rather than scoping out the city's nightlife for any sign of fanged monsters. She sighed again, as if to drive her point home, before speaking. "So . . . what now, kid?"

Abraham's voice broke in then from behind Joss, dripping with an arrogance that Joss couldn't really wrap his head around. "Yes, nephew. Please, enlighten us. What are your plans for this reconnaissance exactly?"

"It's not reconnaissance. It's a stakeout." Joss felt the corner of his mouth twitch. Despite what his uncle Abraham might think, he did know the difference between the two. Reconnaissance was what one did when they watched a certain area, certain people, and gather information about them. A stakeout was that, too, but it also led to action if action is called for.

As if in response to his words, Joss's body became acutely aware of the stake in his back belt loop, hiding under his T-shirt. Apart from Morgan he hadn't told any of the other Slayers about it yet, and was under the assumption that once in a vampire-versus-Slayer showdown, they'd forgive him. Of course, Uncle Abraham would have questions. Lots of questions. And Joss would answer them all. But not now. For now, his stake remained a secret.

Ash chuckled. At a glance from the others, he wiped his grin away. "Sorry. It's just . . . 'stakeout'?

Come on. That's funny. No one else thinks puns are funny? I'm the only one?"

Being that no one else smiled, it had apparently been decided that, yes, Ash was the only person in the group who found Slayer puns funny. Except for Joss, that is, who smiled inwardly at the simple humor. Ash was all right.

When their eyes turned back to Joss, the actor inside of him took center stage. He straightened his shoulders and spoke with a confidence that he didn't feel in the least. "Let's set up a two hundred yard perimeter. Two in the trees. Three on the ground. We'll wait for an hour, then shift locations. By morning, I want a sizable chunk of this park covered."

Cratian and Ash exchanged looks with Paty, and all three fought to hide impressed smiles. Abraham grumbled, "Who gets what position?"

Expecting his uncle's doubtful tone, Joss didn't miss a beat. "Paty and Ash, I want you treetop. Uncle Abraham, Cratian, and myself will cover things from down here. Signal us if you see anything."

Paty blinked. "Signal you? With what, exactly?"

They all looked at him expectantly.

Joss swallowed hard. "Birdcall?"

Much grumbling followed.

Joss blinked, not understanding their reluctance.

"You guys do know how to do birdcalls . . . right?"

Awkward silence and glances around at the various greenery gave Joss his answer. The Slayers could survive for a week on a diet of bark and berries, but not a single one of them had any idea how to mimic the cry of a mourning dove.

Joss cupped his hands together, as if in prayer, and spread his thumbs slightly apart before putting them to his lips and blowing. The Slayers watched in awe as he perfectly mimicked a mourning dove's cry. They practiced for several minutes before moving ahead with their plans. As Ash walked past him, he grinned and spoke under his breath in a tone that sent proud prickles over the back of his neck. "Yes, sir."

Abraham's eyes slanted in suspicion. "Perhaps it would be best for you to be treetop, nephew. You are unarmed, after all."

Joss swallowed hard. Inside his mind, the actor shrugged, at a loss for what to say.

Paty shook her head. "Leave the kid alone, Abraham. You said he was taking point on this little adventure, so let him take point. You can't run everything, despite what you might think. Joss has his reasons for choosing those assignments. And if he's wrong, he'll pay for it. But why not let him learn through experience rather than coddling him like some toddler who's never seen death or felt true pain before?"

Inside Joss's mind, the actor's jaw dropped.

Recovering, Joss simply nodded sternly at his uncle, who set his jaw and disappeared into some nearby bushes. Paty crossed in front of him and scurried up a tree. It took Joss a moment to realize that he was totally alone. After a moment, he walked calmly but alertly through the park until he located a spot just outside of the reach of streetlight in which to hide. He crouched in the darkness, watching as a few tourists wandered through. Soon the park seemed empty. Time passed quickly, and the Slayers changed locations. Every hour they moved to new ground, always with Paty and Ash in the trees, and Abraham, Cratian, and Joss on the ground.

At the sixth hour, bored and exhausted, his leg muscles aching from crouching, standing, and walking, Joss allowed a sliver of doubt to pierce his soul. What had he been thinking? There was nothing here. No vampires. No monsters. Just him and his crew, on a failed mission. With no further clues on how to locate the remaining vampire brothers.

It was over. The Slayer Society would have his head for this failure, and his grandfather would roll over in his grave. And very soon, Joss would join him in his Next Great Adventure.

·20·

CLOSER STILL

Just as Joss was about to break radio silence and call out to his fellow Slayers that the stakeout had been a miserable failure, his cell phone buzzed. Withdrawing it from his pocket, he flipped it open and answered in a hushed voice, full of surprise. "Henry?"

His cousin had never called him on his cell before. Especially after Joss had staked his best friend, Vlad. So he had no idea why he'd call now, unless it was something really important.

"Listen, Joss. I didn't plan on speaking to you ever again, but this is important. Some chick stopped me at the mall here in Stokerton tonight, asking all sorts of questions about you." Henry was all business.

Joss wet his lips and looked around, just in case anyone or anything approached. "A girl? What did she look like?"

"About fifteen. Kinda hot. Weird hair."

Kat. Of that, Joss had no doubt.

Henry paused, and for a brief moment, the edge in his voice softened. "Anyway, she had a weird look in her eye every time I said your name. Like a crazy look. You should watch out for her. Just be careful, okay?"

Joss swallowed a lump that threatened to grow in his throat. "Thanks, Henry. I appreciate it. Maybe next time I'm in town, we could talk, y'know?"

Then the line went dead. His heart sank, and as he returned his phone to his pocket, he wondered if he and Henry would ever be friends, would ever be brothers again. Words entered his mind, words spoken too long ago, and he wondered whether or not they were true.

"Forever, Henry?"

"Forever and ever."

Then Joss heard the sounds of heavy breathing, coupled with the slapping of shoes on pavement. Was this a crazy runner out for some very early morning jogging? He'd wait for them to pass before contacting the other Slayers and telling them his plan was a failure.

But the shoes . . . the runner's shoes sounded off, somehow. Like the soles were harder than the usual running shoe rubber.

He watched the path out of bored curiosity, wondering what kind of person chose to run for entertainment purposes. Running was hard work. Running was something one did with purpose. Not something one would normally choose to do rather than reading a book or watching a movie or playing a video game full of zombie-splattering awesomeness. But to each their own, he supposed.

The breathing sounded heavy, and tinged with panic, sending the tiny hairs on the back of Joss's neck on end. It wasn't the sound of a runner enjoying him- or herself, but the sound of someone fleeing, someone running from something that had frightened them. Every single nerve in Joss's body was on alert as he waited for the runner to come into view. What were they running from? He didn't dare move into a position where he could help until he'd identified the source of their terror.

Then he saw her. A woman in her midthirties, dressed in a miniskirt and sequin-covered bustier, as if she'd been enjoying a night out on the town. Her high heels hit the pavement in desperation, slowing her pace. Joss couldn't help but wonder why she didn't kick them off in order to aid in her flight. Her hair, which looked like it had once been tied in a messy bun, flew wild and free. Her breaths grew more panicked, more shallow as she ran, as if she were quickly running out of steam. But Joss couldn't help her yet. He had to see her tormentor. He had to see who or what was chasing her before he made his move.

She passed by where Joss was crouched in the shadows before she paused to catch her breath. She turned back, eyes on the path, and just as she drew in a sigh of relief, a figure appeared ten yards away. The woman's eyes widened. She froze.

Joss froze, too. He wasn't certain at this distance whether or not the man standing on the path was a vampire or not. He just knew that it was a bad man. A man with ill intentions. A man who meant to harm the woman.

Unless Joss did something about it.

As the man, the creature, whatever he was, advanced on the frightened lady, she seemed held in place by glue. He moved with determination, his steps sure. Closer to her. Closer still. Joss searched the trees above, but couldn't find Paty or Ash anywhere. Where were they? They'd been within eyesight just minutes before. He whistled the birdcall, hoping for some kind of response from his team, but none came.

Joss reached behind him, curling his fingers around his stake. The wood felt warm in his hand. He stepped forward, but just as he was about to be free of the bushes he'd hidden behind, the world disappeared in a swirl of black.

· 21 ·

A SMILE IN THE DARKNESS

Joss's face looked drawn, his forehead creased, with dark circles under his weary eyes. His hair was mussed, his clothes disheveled, and as he sighed, a tiny pink flower petal fluttered down and landed on the surface of the puddle he was staring into, distorting his image. Just as his reflection was smoothing out again, another petal fell, then another. Soon his reflected face was a violent wave of ripples, madly distorted by the falling petals. Then, just as suddenly, the rain of flowers ceased, the petals floating gently to the edges of the puddle. As the puddle stilled, Joss noticed a figure reflected in the puddle, standing beside him, staring at their collective reflection.

Cecile.

Blond curls, blue eyes, happy smile. His baby sister.

He marveled silently at her image for a while, at her perfect curls, at her tan, healthy skin. She was dressed in a yellow sundress, and her toenails had been painted to match its sunny shade. Something about the way she looked—happy, healthy, serene—sent a wave of relief through him, one that ended in a smile of his own. Cecile was fine. She was alive and well and standing right next to him, staring at their images in the puddle below. Regarding her reflection with a nod, he said, "You look very pretty today, Cecile. But where are your shoes?"

Cecile pouted slightly. Adorably. "I don't want to wear shoes, Jossie. They make it hard to run."

Her voice was a song—one that lifted his spirits immeasurably. "What are you running from?"

Running. Someone had been running. He'd heard their footsteps, saw them running. And he was about to do . . . something. What was it?

Cecile's pout sank some, forming a frown tinged with sadness and traced with fear. "The vampires."

Joss's heart skipped a beat then, and he felt his jaw tighten. Whoever he'd seen had been running from vampires, too, hadn't they?

His voice came out more stern that he intended for it to. "You don't have to be afraid of the vampires, Cecile. I'm here now, and I'm going to protect you. Haven't I always been here for you? Haven't I always taken care of you?"

Cecile nodded slowly, then stopped abruptly. "Except . . . except that one time."

Joss furrowed his brow. In the puddle, Cecile furrowed her brow, too. He searched his memories, but couldn't recall a time when he hadn't protected his baby sister. As far as he could recall, he always had. But then, his memories were a bit fuzzy, as if they'd been drawn in chalk and parts had been smudged away—whether by accident or on purpose, he didn't know.

Regarding his sister's reflection, he nodded, forcing a smile. "Well, I'm here now. I'll protect you. From whatever threatens to harm you."

He reached over, taking her hand in his, and gave it a gentle squeeze. In their reflection, Cecile burst out laughing. "How, Jossie?"

Something tickled his wrist, and Joss at last pulled his gaze away from the puddle. He looked down at his hand, the one that was holding hers. A beetle—large, black, and shiny—crawled across his wrist. He shook it away, but another appeared, followed by a worm, a spider, and more ants than Joss could count. He flung his arm wildly to get them off, but Cecile held tight to his hand.

And that's when he noticed her fingernails.

Filth clung to her clawlike nails. The skin around the nail beds was puffy and almost gray in color. Her skin looked raw, rotten. And Joss's heart raced as he raised his eyes to her face.

Her eyes were black tunnels that went on forever. From their depths poured maggots onto her cheeks, the front of her dress, the ground below. She dug her claws into his hand, gripping him to her. And when she spoke, her voice became distorted, with a metallic twinge that sent Joss into a panic so immediate that he nearly screamed. "You can't even protect yourself."

She yanked his arm down, so that he was looking back at his reflection. Maggots poured from her eyes to the puddle. But just before they hit the water, Joss saw something that nearly stole his sanity away forever.

Inside his own mouth were two perfect fangs.

· 22 ·

CURTIS AND SVEN

Darkness curled in around Joss like a blanket, entangling him in its web. Within the darkness was a thick fog, and within that fog was the undeniable fear that he hadn't yet regained consciousness, or worse, that he was on the verge of doing so and the moment he opened his eyes, he'd see Cecile in all of her horrible glory. That was the worst part of these dreams, these nightmares. That Cecile might not just be a pictorial representation of his immense guilt. That she might actually now exist as the monster in his mind.

He allowed himself a few moments in the uncomfortable darkness, hoping like crazy that when he at last opened his eyes, Cecile would not be there. Or if she was, that at least her eyes wouldn't be soulless black tunnels. He'd never admit it—maybe not even to himself—but Joss was scared of her eyes in particular. He worried, on some level of his frightened mind, that he might one day tumble forth, falling into her eyes, plunging into a darkness that had no end. And worse than that, Joss thought that he might deserve such a thing.

But all of these thoughts, these fears, were just something to keep him afloat in the darkness. Nightmares weren't real. And Joss was in no real danger of falling into the black heartless space that was his younger sister's nightmare eyes.

Was he?

At long last, the darkness broke and peeled back from Joss's wakeful mind in layers. As he resurfaced once again into a conscious state, his head began to throb, and memories flooded in. He and the other Slayers had been staking out Central Park. He'd seen something—a vampire, maybe? And that's when everything went dark.

Forcing his eyes open, Joss jumped slightly when all he saw was darkness. The brief, terrifying thought that perhaps he'd already fallen into Cecile's eyes sent his heart racing. But then there was a break in the blackness. A small twinkling. Then another. Stars. He was looking at the night sky.

Turning his head, he saw Paty lying on her side, her wrists and ankles bound with rope, her mouth gagged so tightly that the white cotton was furiously pinching the skin at the corners of her mouth. Her eyes were open, and the moment that she noticed that Joss was awake, she gestured dramatically with her eyes that Joss should look to his left. He did as silently instructed, his eyes widening. To his left the vampire he'd seen chasing the woman earlier was lifting a gag to Cratian's mouth. Beside Cratian sat an already bound Abraham and Ash, who was unconscious and bleeding slightly from his temple. And, to Joss's horror and surprise, beside Ash sat Morgan, with his wrists and ankles bound like the others. In a voice that trembled only slightly, Morgan said, "Do you have any idea what Dorian will do to you if you harm this boy?"

Joss's heart thumped harder. Surely, Morgan was putting on a show. He didn't even know Dorian, just knew *of* Dorian. But it was a great act. Joss almost believed it.

So did the vampire who was gagging him. It paused briefly, then forced the gag into Morgan's mouth, tying it roughly at the back of his head, entangling his hair in the knot. When it spoke, its confident tone was betrayed only by the doubtful twitch in the corner of its mouth. "Dorian will never know."

Joss remained the only Slayer who hadn't yet been gagged. He swallowed a brief moment of doubt and said, "Yes, he will. He knows what you're doing even now, and I can guarantee you, he's not happy about it."

"Really now . . ." The vampire's eyes fogged in a moment of distraction. He twisted his hands in the remaining piece of white cloth—the one he likely planned to gag Joss with—and his entire being became enshrouded in doubt.

Inside Joss's mind, his inner actor took a bow. Every word, every syllable that had crossed his tongue just then had been a convincing lie. Clearly, Dorian was someone to be reckoned with. Someone, perhaps, to fear. Only Joss didn't fear him. Joss was intrigued by him.

A second vampire came into the light then, and ripped the cloth from the other's hands, jarring him. The newcomer's eyes were full of fury. "You fool! They know nothing of Dorian, Sven. Besides, Dorian is in Siberia at the moment. There is no way he could get here in time even if he wanted to. Not that he would ever rescue a group of Slayers. Especially a ragtag band like this one. Stop worrying. You are being tricked by humans."

Something about the way that it had said "humans" gave Joss the impression that he was speaking in the same manner that a farmer might speak about cattle. It's not something that has feelings. It's something to be used for nutrition and dining enjoyment. The thought made Joss's stomach roll with nausea.

The newcomer smiled, turning his attention on Joss. He moved closer, crouching right in front of him. "Does that sicken you, little Slayer? That we view you as nothing more than food and pests?"

Joss set his jaw, refusing the answer. The truth was, it did sicken him. And frighten him. But not in the same way that he was frightened of his sister.

The vampire raised an eyebrow curiously. "Cecile? Now she sounds like a worthy adversary, if I do say so. Those images trapped in your mind . . . the nightmares are unbearable for you. So perhaps it will be an act of kindness when I end your young life."

Joss shook his head quickly, willing the vampire's lips to stop moving, pleading with anything and anyone that the words would stop coming. He couldn't hear them. Wouldn't hear them. Especially from a monster like this. "How are you doing that? How do you know those things?"

The vampire smoothed out the white cloth with his hands, and then rolled it up into a suitable gag before placing it into Joss's mouth. He secured a knot at the back of Joss's head before returning his gaze to Joss's eyes. "We read you like books, human. Sometimes we require information. Sometimes we desire entertainment. But whatever our needs, we can invade your minds at any point, and there is nothing at all that you can do to stop us."

But there was one thing. Joss could kill them. And once they were dead, his mind would be his again. His alone.

The vampire's eyes darkened as he stood again. "You can try, little Slayer. You can try."

The other vampire, the one called Sven, seemed to regain his composure. He stepped forward, eyeing each of the Slayers with disdain. "You all—all but Abraham, that is—question why my brother and I haven't yet killed you. The answer is simple. You deserve punishment. You deserve sheer terror and pain. And we will not rest until those things are appropriately administered."

Joss glimpsed a tattoo on each of their left arms. It matched the one that had been on Boris and Kaige. Brothers, all four.

Both vampires snapped their eyes to Joss then at the mention of their brothers in his thoughts. He hadn't yet been truly afraid of the notion of telepathy. But at that moment, Joss was afraid. He couldn't hide anything from an enemy who was capable of invading his mind, of reading his thoughts. They could predict every move and countermove that he could ever offer. They could uncover his deepest fears, his greatest desires, and use those things against him. How could he fight something that had that kind of power?

He couldn't.

The vampire who hadn't shared his name yet, the one Joss knew to be Curtis, spoke then, his tone darkening. Perhaps in grief. "It is a sad day when any vampire succumbs to the great emptiness that is death. But to be brought to that finality by a child . . ."

Sven took a bold step toward Joss, shaking his long finger in Joss's face. "You will suffer most of all, young one."

Curtis kicked Abraham hard in the ribs. Abraham cried out, his injured yelp muffled by the gag in his mouth. The vampire bent closer to his face then and grinned. "We're going to play a game, old man."

"Yes. On to our game, shall we?" Sven chuckled. "As retribution for the murder of our dear brothers, we demand balance. And balance can only be achieved by a life for a life."

A memory flashed briefly in Joss's mind. A teacher he'd had in the fifth grade, lecturing him on vengeance. He'd shaken his head in disappointment and said to Joss, *"An eye for an eye and a tooth for a tooth will only leave you blind and toothless, Joss."*

At the time, he thought it was the dumbest thing he'd ever heard. But now it was starting to make a little more sense. Maybe, Joss shuddered, in the literal sense. He might not get out of this with eyes or teeth.

Curtis grinned. Maybe he could sense the Slayer's fear. Or maybe, Joss thought with horror, he was merely expressing his joy at the idea of Joss being left with every tooth ripped from his mouth, each eye plucked from its socket. An image matching that description flashed through Joss's mind and he gasped. The other Slayers sat absurdly still. Finally, Ash moved slightly, groaning like he was in pain. When he finally opened his eyes, he struggled, panicking against his bonds. Then he darted a glance around the clearing. As he caught sight of the Slayers, his muscles seemed to stop twitching in fear, but the fear moved from his limbs to his eyes. The vampires smiled down on him, drinking in his terror as if it were a fine wine. When Ash had settled down, Curtis continued to speak. "You, as our dear departed brothers Boris and Kaige were, will be hunted. When you are captured, each of you will be killed. You'll be dinner. You'll be our food, our playthings. We will not show mercy. We will not give kindness. We will chase you. We will catch you. And we will kill you."

Joss searched the clearing, but found no way of escape, no tool that could assist he and his Slayer team to get out of this situation. His stake was long gone, and he was betting that theirs were as well. He couldn't think of any possible escape. Hopelessness sank into the pit of his stomach like a dropped stone. Heavy. Solid.

Curtis ruffled Joss's hair and in a mocking tone said, "There, there, little Slayer boy. All hope is not lost. I tell you what. If you can make it to the city streets, I'll let you go free and hunt you later. A three-day head start. What do you say?"

"Bartering?" A girl's voice intruded, followed by a clucking tongue. "Curtis, I had no idea you were so open-minded about the subject of negotiation."

Joss whipped his head around. It was Kat, come for vengeance at last. It had to be.

Curtis's head snapped up, as did his brother's. But it was Sven who spoke, in a shaking voice, with wide, fearful eyes. "Em . . . I . . . we . . . no. Not at all. We weren't . . . I wasn't—"

The girl stepped into the light. This girl lacked Kat's kind face, her stubborn chin. She was dressed in black skinny jeans, purple and black Converse high-tops, and a purple T-shirt that featured Count Chocula. On her right wrist were twenty or so thin, black rubber bracelets, as well as a thick black bracelet that read simply, BITE ME. Her eyes seemed bright even in the darkness. And when she turned her gaze on Joss, he froze.

He'd seen her before. In a photograph that Morgan had given him. This was Em. He was sure of it.

A sly smile formed on her lips, and though she looked every bit a teenage girl, Joss was certain in her presence that she was anything but. The girl standing before him wasn't a girl at all, but a vampire. It was in her eyes, that knowledge of ages. She had lived, died, experienced, killed, and done everything in between. Except, he thought with a strange twinge of sadness, she'd never empathized. She was evil. Sad. Alone.

A hint of anger flashed through her expression as she looked at Joss. But when she spoke, it wasn't to him, but to Curtis and Sven. "Give no quarter, gentlemen. I want these Slayers dead and bloodless by sunrise. Play your games, but if even one escapes, you'll pay for it with your lives. I've put up with enough nonsense from you and your brothers feasting in the open. My patience has worn thin. Now kill them. And make the young one hurt."

She turned and exited the clearing. Without a word, Curtis and Sven began removing the Slayers' gags. Joss waited for one of them to speak, to bite, to do something, but the Slayers sat calmly, with their mouths closed, eyes forward. Sven tugged Joss's gag from his mouth before untying it. After he did, he grinned in Joss's face. "We'll take special care with you, little Slayer boy. Em wants you to hurt, so we'll kill you last. After we make you suffer, of course. That way, we can take our time."

He opened his mouth then, and Joss shuddered to see two long fangs elongating inside of his mouth.

"Sven! Help me untie them," Curtis barked at his brother, sounding more than a little impatient to get started. He also sounded less amused than he had with the entire situation before Em had shown up. It had been like a game before, but now it was more like a chore, and he seemed to want it over as quickly and as efficiently as possible.

One by one, the brothers untied each of the Slayers, starting with Paty, and once they did, each Slayer took off into the darkness without a word. Joss couldn't shake the feeling that he was being left behind. It felt very much like a case of every man for himself, rather than the family bond they'd shared last summer, after his long and grueling training. He wouldn't abandon them, though. Because if Joss was anything, he was loyal, dutiful, and would do anything to protect those that he cared about.

Just as Sven untied his ankles, followed by his wrists, Joss stood as calmly as he could, regarded each of the vampires with a glare, and stepped quietly from the clearing. The moment he was cloaked in darkness, he took off in a sprint. He had to get away, far away, and find some way to hide. Hide his scent. Hide his thoughts. There had to be a way.

Just as he was rounding a particularly large oak tree, a phantom arm reached out from behind its immense trunk and grabbed him by the shoulder, yanking him closer. Joss gasped, but once he was on the other side of the tree, Abraham pressed a finger to his own lips, instructing Joss to stay quiet. Then Abraham leaned closer to Joss and whispered, "Bite your tongue. They can't break through the steady pain to read your thoughts."

Then he placed his finger on his lips again before moving off in a southern direction, eyes darting this way and that. Joss furrowed his brow. Could it really be that simple? If that were true, a Slayer could easily feed misinformation to the vampire that was hunting him. And if so, he might just get out of this with his eyes and teeth intact.

It also totally explained why the other Slayers had been so quiet. He was the only one giving the vampires access to his thoughts at all in the clearing.

He bit his tongue between his molars, clamping down until there was a steady ache, then he moved in the same direction as his uncle. They had to find the others and get out of here and somewhere safe before Curtis and Sven found them.

No, Joss thought. They had to get the jump on the vampire brothers and take them out. Or else Curtis and Sven would go on hunting their Slayer crew forever.

They had to kill, or they would die. Joss thought about Kaige, and about the way his blood had felt as it splashed onto Joss's skin. The act had sickened him. But he had no choice. He had to take these lives to protect those he cared about.

And he would do so by any means necessary.

· 23 ·

THE IMMINENT DEATH OF AN INVISIBLE BOY

Joss moved through the park as fast and as quietly as he was able, the night air brushing his hair back away from his face, the early dew moistening his ankles as he ran. As far as he could tell, no one and nothing was in pursuit of him. There were no sounds, other than the ones he made and the usual sounds of night in a park, with the echoes of city life as their accompaniment. And no unusual scents filled his nostrils. But the undeniable feeling, the inescapable sensation that he was being followed by someone—by something—refused to be shaken from his mind. The tiny hairs on the back of his neck stood on end, and he couldn't tell if the feeling was just a lingering response to his recent interaction with Curtis and Sven or if it was his intuition kicking in, telling him that it was either time to pick up the pace and get his butt moving, or turn and face the horrors that had come for him.

In this past year's biology class, Joss had learned all about a human's fight-or-flight response to fear. He'd decided at the time, and was reminded of it now, that one should always choose flight before they gave fight a try, in situations where one was not entirely prepared to fight. His uncle might have called him a coward for believing such a thing, for even thinking it, but at the moment, Joss didn't care. He needed some distance, and some time to develop a solid plan of attack, before facing down two vampires the likes of Curtis and Sven. So he kept on running, with no vampires and no Slayers in sight, not knowing where he was going or what he was going to do once he got there. It felt good to run. He felt almost free.

Abraham had disappeared into the darkness. Maybe he knew precisely where to go and exactly what to do, but Joss hadn't followed him, and he wasn't certain that his uncle would have wanted him to. He was pretty certain—even though he hoped that no one would ever quote him on that—that Abraham would have preferred that he break away from his uncle's lead, and find his own way. So Joss ran through the night, and tried to think of when and where would be the best place to stop.

His lungs eventually began to burn, and when they did, and that horrible feeling that he was being watched had passed, Joss slowed his steps and came to a stop near the trunk of a small maple tree. He took a few seconds to calm his breathing and examine the area around him for any sign of his vampire pursuers. To his great and immediate relief, there were none. Just shadows and darkness, and the rather comforting images that nature had to provide.

To his left, a bird began its call, but no bird that Joss was familiar with. After its coos had become cries for a few minutes, the bird morphed into Morgan, who stage-whispered, "Are you stupid? It's me! What bird on earth sounds like that?! Get up here!"

Joss looked up, shaking his head at his assumption. Morgan was perched in the lower hanging branches of a nearby oak. Joss climbed the tree with a precision that he'd been lacking before last summer. As he shimmied out onto the same branch that Morgan was perched on, Joss whispered back. "Sorry. You were really convincing. I thought you were a bird. Just one I didn't recognize."

Morgan's eyes were scanning the area below, his voice sounding only slightly distracted from the subject at hand. "I'll take that as a compliment, little brother, but unless you see me sprouting feathers out of my butt, don't believe it."

He wondered if that was Morgan's way of saying that he shouldn't take anything for granted, but the thought flickered out of his mind just as quickly as it had entered. Morgan was not the judgmental type. Not like Joss's uncle. Not like Joss's father.

His father.

The image of his dad entered his mind immediately, and he wondered if he would ever see his dad again, or if they would ever be the family that they had been before Cecile had been murdered. He wanted that more than anything—to have his dad back again—even more than he wanted vengeance for what had happened to his baby sister. And he couldn't help but wonder at that moment if he ever would. Would he die tonight? Would his parents soon be attending the funeral of their only remaining child? Would they cry at that funeral? Or had they become so empty, so devoid of sadness and loss that their tears had dried completely, leaving nothing for the mourning of their only son?

He hoped that there would be more than blank stares and emptiness. He hoped—guiltily—that there would be at least a few tears left for the son, the way that there had been so many for their daughter.

It hurt him, to think these things, to feel these

things, but what it boiled down to at the moment was that all Joss really wanted was to be seen by his parents. To be recognized and loved and, damn it, revered. At the very least, he wanted to be noticed. He was sick and too tired of being the Invisible Boy. He wanted to be their son again, and if he had to die tonight to be just that . . . then that, he supposed, was exactly what he had to do. Gone were the days of being invisible. Long live the era of their son, the Slayer.

Even though they most likely would never know the importance of his position.

"What are you doing here, Morgan? Abraham said you weren't allowed to come with us."

Morgan shook his head sadly. "I had to come. I couldn't stay there, poking at a dead body, wondering if I'd just let you all march to your deaths without me. And I know what your uncle thinks about me, that my loyalty is compromised, that I'll likely eventually divulge information to my brother, endangering our crew, and at greater risk, the Society itself. But I swear to you, little brother, my loyalty is absolutely to you, Paty, Ash, Cratian, and Abraham. I would never betray any of you, and I would never endanger the Slayer Society's existence."

Joss listened, but couldn't help but wonder why Morgan would choose this moment to express his loyalty to their cause. Perhaps he thought he might not get another chance. Or perhaps he thought that no one in the clan would listen to him the way that Joss would.

Or perhaps, Joss thought with a suspicious worry, Morgan viewed him as gullible, an easy target for someone who was hell-bent on helping the vampires learn as much as they could about the Slayer Society.

And maybe, as loathe as Joss was to admit it, based on Joss's past performance, Morgan might have been wise to think that Joss was the perfect target.

"I just wanted you to know that." Morgan's voice trailed off, leaving them with only the sounds of night filling their perked ears. Joss felt a bit guilty about not having replied. He'd wanted to say something, but wasn't sure what to say, exactly. Wasn't saying nothing at all better than saying something stupid or inane? So Joss had remained silent and hoped that Morgan would understand.

After several minutes of awkward silence between the two, Morgan gestured to the scene below them with his chin and whispered, "What do you see, little brother?"

Joss looked around at the moonlight-filled park and shrugged. "Just the park. Why?"

Then Morgan threw him a meaningful glance and gestured again. This time, his words hit Joss like a gentle slap upside the head. "But what do you *see*?"

He looked again, this time not as a teenage kid, but as a fierce slaying machine. His eyes scanned the landscape for any sign of life. After a moment, he had it. "Fresh tracks in the soft ground roughly twenty yards out. Sneakers, size twelve, maybe thirteen. Judging by the size, probably male. Judging by the indent, likely about two hundred pounds or so."

"Vampire?" Morgan's tone was that of a teacher once again, the way that it had been in the Catskills last summer. Joss liked hearing him like this.

With his eyes locked on the imprints in the ground, Joss shook his head with confidence. "Human. The footfalls are too heavy to be a vampire. Vamps, despite their weight, move lightly over the ground. They're masters of stealth."

"What else?"

Joss scanned his eyes over the landscape, but saw nothing. His eyes fell once more on the footprints he'd noticed before, and when he looked at them this time, he noticed something that he hadn't before. He sat up anxiously. It was difficult to keep his voice quiet. "There's another footprint inside that footprint. Size ten loafers. Barely a dent. That's our man."

He looked at Morgan, who was beaming with pride. Joss grinned. "Or monster. Depending on who you ask."

Morgan patted him on the back and sighed. "But

now we have to do something that I really hate to do. We have to get out of this tree and away from our cover so that we can track the monster through the woods. Be careful down there, Joss. We'll be completely exposed. If they find us before we can take them out, odds are we're dead. Ticked off vampires are a lot harder to kill, for some reason."

Joss furrowed his brow. "But there are only two of them. And everyone broke off away from the group! I don't understand why we didn't stay together. There's strength and safety in numbers. It says so in the field guide."

"Kid, not everything in life can be summed up neatly in a paragraph. No book has all of the answers. Not even the really good ones. You have to find the answers for yourself sometimes." Without another word, Morgan shimmied down the tree and Joss followed, keeping a watchful eye on the area around them. They made it to the footprints and began to follow them, but after thirty yards of steady tracks, they disappeared. Joss furrowed his brow and looked around. Two small branches from a nearby bush had been bent back, as if someone had pushed them away forcefully. And Joss was betting that the person who'd done it wore size twelve, maybe size thirteen sneakers.

He stepped away for Morgan to investigate and, pressed into the soft earth on the other side of the bush, was another footprint, matching the ones they'd been following. Inside, so faint that Joss had to squint in the moonlight in order to see it, was the imprint of a second shoe. Morgan let him take the lead and they followed the tracks for what felt like maybe a quarter of a mile, deep into the heart of Central Park.

But then the tracks stopped.

Not the human's tracks, but the vampire's. They were nowhere to be seen. After Boris, Joss knew that vampires were capable of hovering, but he and Morgan had carefully searched the trees to no avail. The vampire in question was simply gone.

Morgan chewed his bottom lip nervously, his eyes moving over their surroundings again and again in every direction. He looked more worried than Joss had ever seen him before. "Let's backtrack, little brother. See if we missed something."

But as they moved back through the woods, they must have gotten turned around, because before Joss knew it, they were standing near a rocky outcropping. A fountain stood at its center, splashing water on the ground below. Morgan looked around, trying to figure out exactly how they'd gotten off track, but all Joss could focus on was the silhouette of something that was perched on the fountain's edge.

White and black feathers, large eyes, and a shape that was impossible to mistake for anything else. A large owl stood on the edge of the fountain, its huge eyes locked on Joss and Morgan. Was it watching them? No, that was crazy. Why would an owl be watching them? Wouldn't it be more inclined to watch field mice or small rabbits? But still. Joss couldn't shake the feeling that the bird was staring at him, and not just because he was an interesting shape in the darkness.

He nudged Morgan and pointed at the owl. "Check it out."

Morgan glanced at the owl and shrugged, his eyes returning quickly to their search of the treetops. "So what? You've never seen an owl before?"

Of course he'd seen an owl before. But this one seemed . . . different, somehow. He couldn't explain it. "Do they usually stare like that?"

Morgan looked at it again, but this time, Joss noticed a visible shift in his fellow Slayer's mood. Morgan tensed and whispered harshly to Joss, "Get out of here. Now."

Just as Joss was turning to do as he'd been told, Morgan broke into a run and dove at the offending bird. The owl flapped its wings, leaping from the fountain's edge to flight. But its flight was short-lived. Morgan met it in midair with his stake raised high. But as the bird flew, Joss found his feet cemented to the ground in shock. The owl transformed as it moved through the air, growing larger. It lost its wings first.

They became the arms of a man. Its head followed, giving it all of the features of a man, though its eyes were the last feature to go. Joss recognized Curtis immediately. He could change into an owl? Joss's heart raced in fear. Vampires could hide anywhere. No one was safe.

As Curtis's chest transformed, he twisted, digging his enormous claws into Morgan's torso. Flipping quickly, he tossed Morgan into the outcropping in a bloody heap. Morgan's stake flew through the air, landing several feet from his unconscious form. When Curtis landed on the ground, he was no longer an owl, but the fierce vampire that Joss had been sent here to kill. He looked at Morgan with a murderous gleam in his eye and moved forward to finish him off.

Joss broke into a run, jumping into the air. His feet connected with the side of Curtis's head, knocking him back into the pool of water that surrounded the fountain. Curtis skidded across the surface of the water, coming to a halt in a crouched and ready position, eyes locked on Joss. Joss's heart was pounding in his ears as terror filled his every pore. "Slayer," he hissed. "That is the last mistake that you will ever make."

Curtis lunged at him, and Joss reached for Morgan's stake, but Curtis was too fast. Then Curtis gnashed his teeth at Joss, and all Joss could think to do was to block the attack, to stop Curtis from biting or hitting him. He blocked again and again, not realizing that he'd been backing up until his back met solidly with a tree trunk. Curtis pulled back his arm and grinned. "Slayer, I've decided that I'm going to rip your heart out *before* I eat it."

Curtis shot his hand forward, aiming for the center of Joss's chest. He meant to break through Joss's rib cage with his bare hand and tear out the tender organ that sustained Joss's life.

But in a moment of panic, Joss relaxed all of his muscles and fell to the ground, just dodging the blow. Curtis's arm entered the tree trunk instead. He said something loudly in a language that Joss couldn't understand, and pulled back on his arm, but for the moment, he was stuck. Joss knew he didn't have much time, so he pummeled Curtis's ribs with one fist, hoping to subdue him long enough to grab Morgan's stake with his free hand. But just as grabbed the stake, it was knocked to the ground by an unseen force.

Joss cursed and turned around to see Sven, his eyes furious slits, his chest heaving in breaths that suggested that he'd been running just a few seconds before. Joss's heart beat once before he dove after Morgan's stake. Sven was on him before his fingers even brushed against the wood, snapping Joss's left arm like a twig. Pain lit up Joss's entire world and he screamed at the brightness of it all, at the excruciating hurt. Clutching his useless arm to his side, Joss fell to the ground. Then Sven dove toward him. In a moment of sheer desperation, Joss reached out with his good arm to find something, anything, to defend himself with. His fingers closed over something familiar and warm, and just as Sven was falling on him, mouth wide, fangs exposed, Joss brought the stake back to his chest and forced it upward, piercing Sven's heart.

Immediately, he shoved Sven's corpse from his body, pulling Morgan's stake free. He stood and approached Curtis with a determined step. Curtis was struggling against the tree, his arm almost free, cursing at Joss in that strange language. But Joss didn't care. He only cared about the reason he was doing any of this. He only cared about right and wrong. He gripped the stake in his fist and whispered, "For you, Cecile. Every time."

As he thrust the stake forward, Curtis howled. The silver pierced his skin and plunged deep into Curtis's chest. Then Curtis went still.

He withdrew Morgan's stake and noted with interest that his fingers weren't shaking at all. He'd killed the beast with a steady hand.

From behind him came the sound of someone clapping. He turned to see Ash, Morgan, Paty, Cratian, and Abraham watching him with shining, proud eyes. Abraham offered him a nod before putting his cell phone to his ear. "This is Abraham. We need a cleanup on the southern end of Central Park."

Morgan limped over to him and gave him a brotherly hug before looking down on Curtis's remains. "One thing's for sure, little brother. The next time I get attacked by an oversized canary, I'm calling you."

·24·

NIGHT HOTEL

"**Y**ou are so slow! Come on, Joss. Half of this stuff is for you! Pick up the pace." Paty was walking in front of Joss, heading down the sidewalk toward the brownstone. In her arms were three boxes, and looped over her arms were four big bags of clothing, split between each arm. Joss was lugging three bags and two boxes—but with one arm in a cast. The boxes were piled so high that he almost couldn't see Paty in front of him. She had claimed that the shopping trip was a celebration, and that the clothes were gifts for Joss. But only two pairs of pants and three shirts were his. Most of the shopping had been for Paty. And now Joss was her injured pack mule.

To his dismay, his toes caught on an uneven bit of sidewalk and Joss tripped. He caught himself before he fell, but the packages went down, falling around him in thumps. Joss grumbled, but a moment later, Morgan appeared, chuckling. "Doing a bit of shopping, little brother?"

Joss rolled his eyes. "More like Paty's shopping. I'm just carrying."

Morgan grabbed most of the boxes and three of the bags. "One word of advice, kid? Never go shopping with a girl. Even one who carries a stake."

As Morgan moved along after Paty, Joss gathered the remaining packages, noted Morgan's advice, and followed suit. It was time to head back to the brownstone, time to pack, time to get ready, and time to go home. The event filled Joss with mixed feelings. On one hand, he was proud of himself, of them, for having taken care of the vampire brothers as assigned. On the other, the only thing awaiting him at home were his parents, and neither of them seemed to have much of a place for Joss in their lives anymore. It was difficult to look forward to spending time with people who treated him like the Invisible Boy. It was impossible to face the fact that his parents would never change. Cecile's death had shaped them into something that Joss couldn't comprehend, and in ways, didn't want to comprehend. He just wanted to have something to look forward to whenever he set foot in those four walls he referred to as "home."

As he walked, trailing a bit behind Paty and Morgan under the weight of Paty's shopping bags, someone fell into step beside him, their paces matching immediately. He turned his head and blinked, a bit surprised to see Dorian walking along beside him. The corner of Dorian's mouth lifted in a small smile. "It's good to see you, young sir."

Joss glanced at Paty and Morgan, but they seemed completely oblivious to Dorian's presence. The strange sensation came over him that Dorian was somehow making them not notice him. He looked back at Dorian, wondering if Dorian had ever controlled his awareness in that way. The idea that anyone could have that kind of power frightened him. Even if Dorian seemed relatively harmless. It was bad enough that vampires could tap into the dark recesses of a human's mind and hear every whisper of thought that they had. It was worse that Dorian might be able to do more.

Because he was more than a vampire. Joss just didn't know how much more, or what that meant, exactly.

Dorian kept his eyes straight ahead, as if he knew where they were headed and was totally okay with that. "I thought we might discuss where exactly I got the stake that I gifted you with, and why exactly I gave it to you. I believe we've put off this conversation for long enough."

Joss stopped walking, stopped moving, stopped breathing for a moment, and turned to face Dorian, who mimicked his movements perfectly. It sent a chill up Joss's spine. "I was hoping you'd say that, Dorian. So . . . go ahead. I'm all ears. Tell me about the stake."

Joss looked up the street to where Paty and Morgan were still walking, and then back to Dorian, who'd already made his way half a block.

Without as much as a brief pause in his steps, Dorian continued his trek down the street, calling over his shoulder to a bewildered Joss, who still had no idea how Dorian knew that he even had nightmares, let alone wanted to discuss them. "Come, my friend. Let us talk."

Joss hurried to follow after him, not knowing how he'd explain his absence to Morgan and Paty later, but too eager to understand how Dorian had come about Ernst's stake, and why he'd given it to Joss, when the Slayer Society had not yet deemed him worthy of owning the instrument. He caught up to Dorian a block over, and silently, they made their way to a boutique hotel on a bustling street. The sign read simply NIGHT.

The doorman at Night Hotel opened the door for

Joss and smiled. Just after Joss stepped into the lobby, Dorian appeared behind him, walking with him, as if they'd arrived here together on purpose. The doorman's smile grew. "Good to see you back, sir. I see you found your friend. Shall I send up something to drink in a few minutes? The house red, perhaps?"

Dorian smiled and shook his head. "I believe that Mountain Dew will do just fine for my young friend here, Albert."

Albert smiled. "Of course, sir. Anything."

Standing sentinel in the black-on-black lobby were two large, white pillars. Black leather chairs filled the space, kept company by smidges of white in the animal skin chairs and orchids adorning the shiny glass tables. The carpet was black with white, old English monograms. *N* for "Night." It was a cool hotel—old and funky, but so very modern— and he hadn't yet left the lobby.

As they passed the front desk on their way to the elevators, a woman in her early twenties flashed Dorian a smile. "Good afternoon, sir. Shall I send up some of the house re—"

"No. Thank you." Dorian held up a hand, cutting off her words. Joss thought that maybe the house red wine was the best thing that the hotel had. It had to be. Otherwise, why would they be practically shoving it down Dorian's throat?

He slowed his steps. House red. That was what the bartender at V Bar had offered Joss. It was a code word. For blood. Because Dorian was absolutely a vampire.

And Joss's stake was nowhere to be found. He was unarmed, and in the company of an enemy. What was he thinking?

As they stood waiting for the elevator, Joss wondered exactly what he was doing. He didn't know Dorian at all, and yet here he was, following this strange vampire upstairs to his hotel room. As the door opened, music by The Cure pouring out from inside, Joss hesitated. Dorian stepped inside, holding the door for him. After a moment that seemed to drag on into eternity, Dorian lowered his head, locking his eyes with Joss's. "Joss. It's okay. You have nothing to fear from me."

Had Joss heard right? It had almost sounded like Dorian had placed emphasis on the words 'you' and 'me.' As if Dorian might have something to fear from Joss.

Joss debated turning around and running from the hotel, but something in his chest settled, and a calm washed over him. Before he knew he was doing it, Joss stepped inside the elevator, and they were on their way to the penthouse floor. Beside him, Dorian smiled. "I'm glad you're here, Joss. We have so much to discuss. I'm not one to interfere unnecessarily, but this is important. More important than anyone realizes. Even you."

"Even me?" Joss furrowed his brow in confusion. It all seemed so ominous. So surreal. And he still wasn't sure what he was doing here, or why he was going along with this little field trip, when he knew that Dorian was a monster.

The elevator door opened, revealing a small foyer. It was wallpapered in something that resembled black and white speckled fur. To the left and the right were locked doors. Dorian explained, "There are two penthouse suites. I normally stay in the one to your left, the one with rooftop access, but important guests are at the hotel tonight, so I'm calling the smaller penthouse home for now."

Joss stared in disbelief. "You . . . *own* this place?"

Dorian pulled out a key card and swiped it through the reader of the door on the right, smiling all the while. When he pushed the door open, Joss almost gasped. The walls inside were papered in black and white, featuring large, ornate thistles. The carpeting was rich black, and the room contained only an oversized black leather chair, reading lamp, and a small desk with a computer on it. It was the strangest hotel room that Joss had ever seen—not that he'd seen many.

Dorian led him out onto the balcony and closed

the door behind them. Moments later, room service served them with a silver ice bucket, holding a two liter of Mountain Dew, and a single long stem glass. The man poured the glass full and handed it to Joss before turning to leave. Joss took a sip, and then looked at Dorian. "Don't you want any?"

"I never drink . . ." He took a breath, one that felt like it went on for ages. ". . . Mountain Dew."

They sat there, in the warm breeze, and Joss emptied his glass and said, "Why did you bring me here, Dorian? What is this?"

Dorian stood and moved to the edge of the balcony, peering over it to the traffic below. "You know what I am, Joss."

Joss's heart picked up its pace. Again, he thought of his stake and how much he wished he had it with him now. "Of course I do. You're a vampire."

Dorian's shoulders lifted and fell slowly, as if he were taking a very deep breath. When he spoke, Joss could just barely make out what he was saying. "And yet I live."

At first, Joss raised an eyebrow. Live? Was he expecting Joss to kill him? Hoping, maybe?

Dorian turned back to him briefly. Just long enough to direct his gaze to a small table near the door. On top of it lay a wooden stake. Joss's stake. He picked it up.

Dorian looked up at the sky for but a moment, but

when he turned back to face Joss, the glass dropped from Joss's fingers, crashing on the floor between his feet.

Fangs filled Dorian's mouth. He bared them at Joss, growling. "Go on! Do it, Joss! For both of us! Get it over with!"

Joss shook his head, but he wasn't sure what message he was trying to convey. He was a Slayer. Dorian was a vampire with a death wish. What part of this was he having a problem with? Dorian nodded slowly. "Please, Joss. Please. I grow so very weary of all the tasks that lay before me. End this. Now."

Joss swallowed hard, resisting the urge to grip his stake. Not yet, anyway. "Where did you get my stake, Dorian?"

Dorian's fangs retreated, his shoulders slumped, as if in defeat. "Initially, from your great-great-great-grandfather. He was a nice man, if not a little on the stubborn side. He tried to kill me, and as he lay dying, he reached for his stake, to hold it as a small comfort as he passed from this life into oblivion. I handed it to him, watched him die, and then packed up the kit. The moment I touched it, I saw a face in my mind."

Dorian stepped closer, looking as if he were examining Joss's face the way one might examine a painting. Joss couldn't help but wonder what Dorian saw between each brushstroke. Then Dorian stepped back with an apologetic glance. "Your face. I knew that I would find you someday, and that when I did, I had to give you that kit. I had to give you that stake. And then, once I realized that it had been taken from you, I knew that I would have to return it to your hand, to arm you once again with the tool that you will eventually use to take my life."

Joss shook his head. He reached for his stake, but slid it into place at his back without so much as pointing it in Dorian's direction. His words were merely a whisper in the night. "But . . . why? You're a vampire. I'm a Slayer. It makes no sense for you to help me."

A sadness settled into the corners of Dorian's mouth then as he looked at Joss. "Because, my young friend. You're the boy that I've been dreaming about. You're the boy who's going to end my life. And I am an impatient fool."

Joss's heart sank, betraying him.

Even though he trusted Dorian's words—and oh, how he hated the fact that he did, not knowing whether or not that trust had been put in place by himself or Dorian—he thought about where he was, and the fact that if he screamed, he wasn't sure anyone would come running to help him. After all, Dorian owned Night Hotel. He was fairly certain that the staff would do just about anything to protect him and his interests. Swallowing hard, he looked into Dorian's eyes and ran a nervous hand over the back of his neck before speaking. "Dorian, are . . . are you going to kill me?"

A hint of a smile touched the corners of Dorian's lips. He didn't seemed surprised to hear Joss's words, merely amused. As if he'd just listened to a joke that had tickled his funny bone many years ago. When the smile finally faded, he shook his head slowly at Joss, as if his next words were the most important that Joss would ever hear. "No. But I am going to warn you. Em knows who you are now, and knows that you still live. She will not touch you while I am at home in my fair city, but that won't protect you once you leave. She will stop at nothing to make you suffer. You must be extremely careful, my friend."

Dorian looked at him for a long, silent moment before turning away. His next words were a whisper. "Now go."

Joss stood. He crossed the room, moved into the hall, and was all the way to the lobby before he realized that he'd done just what Dorian had told him to.

He felt hollow. He felt alone.

·25·

HOMEWARD BOUND

That afternoon, Joss sat in a hard blue chair that was bolted to a row of other hard, blue chairs in LaGuardia Airport, waiting for the ominous voice from above to tell him it was time to board his plane, and travel to a place where he ceased to be Joss McMillan, Vampire Slayer, and became Joss McMillan, Invisible Boy. The drastic shift that he was about to experience, not to mention the conversation he'd just had with Dorian, left him sinking down in his seat, unwilling to be the pleasant actor that had flown here just two and a half months before. He didn't smile, didn't make eye contact with passersby. He merely sat, his heart breaking over two very different things, and waited for the voice to tell him it was time to go.

He could understand being upset over his parents and their treatment of him—even though he really didn't get why they'd changed so drastically after the loss of Cecile. But he couldn't quite understand why Dorian's admission had bothered him so much. So Dorian had dreams about him in which Joss staked him. So what? Why did that bother Joss? He was a Slayer. And frankly, if Joss ended up staking him sometime in the future, then it probably meant that Dorian deserved it, right? Right.

So why did it trouble Joss so deeply?

Because, the tiny voice in the back of his mind prodded, deep down, whether or not Joss wanted to admit it, he liked Dorian. Despite the fact that Dorian was a monster.

The idea that Joss really liked a vampire, one who'd given him absolutely no reason at all to despise him, sickened Joss. He would have given just about anything at that moment for Dorian to be something else, something other than the bloodsucking monster that he was.

That Vlad was. That Sirus had been.

And Joss was going to kill him. He was destined to kill Dorian, and the truly twisted thing was, he wasn't at all certain that he wanted to. Maybe that was because he didn't like the idea of having his actions decided for him. He wasn't sure. But it certainly didn't sit well on his mind.

He couldn't tell anyone, of course. He couldn't tell his uncle or the other Slayers about any of this—except for maybe Morgan. In fact, Morgan might understand his situation better than anyone, what with having a vampire for a brother. Straightening in his seat just a little, Joss made a mental note to speak to Morgan about it the next time they saw each other and picked up his carry-on bag. The ominous voice from above bellowed out his flight number and his group number for boarding, so Joss stood up and shuffled into line with the other passengers.

He'd just slid his small carry-on under the seat in front of him and buckled up for the ride when his cell phone buzzed inside his pocket, as if reminding him that it was just about time to turn off and put away all electronic devices. Joss withdrew it, and wasn't at all surprised to see a text from Kat.

I LEARNED A LOT ABOUT YOU THIS SUMMER, JOSS. AFTER I GET BACK FROM SIBERIA, YOU AND I ARE GOING TO FACE OFF. I HOPE YOU'RE READY.—K

Joss took a deep breath and typed in a return message before hitting SEND.

READY. NOT WILLING. BUT READY. IF YOU INSIST, KAT.

Before he could put his phone away, it rang. Raising an eyebrow at the number on the screen, he flipped it open, pressing it to his ear. "Uncle Abraham. Did I forget something?"

A strange tightness settled into his chest. He liked his uncle, but was still slightly afraid of him. He never knew what to expect when Abraham opened his mouth. And Abraham never called him. Ever. In fact, if Paty hadn't added his number to Joss's contact list last summer, Joss wouldn't have recognized the number at all. He slid down in his seat a little and waited for the tightness in his chest to subside.

"No, Joss, but I'm afraid that I did." Abraham's voice sounded warmer in tone than it had all summer. The flight attendant waved a hand at Joss and pointed to the phone as if to tell him that it was time to put his phone away, but Joss held up a finger in response. He needed two seconds for this phone call. Besides, the guy across the aisle was still using his laptop. Couldn't she go bug him? "I didn't get a chance to thank you, nephew."

Joss didn't mention it, but there were many chances to say something while they were at the brownstone. They'd shared two dinners after fighting off the vampires in the park. Why couldn't he say anything then? But then, Joss was feeling a bit shocked that his uncle had called at all, let alone to thank him for something, so his mind was all over the place.

Abraham said, "You were given a task that, to date, none in the Society had been able to complete. And you pulled it off. I'm proud of you. I just wanted to say that."

Joss sat back in his seat, his jaw dropping into his lap. Compliments and gratitude were two things that just didn't seem to fit with his uncle's personality. Being on the receiving end of both combined was enough to send Joss into a state of utter shock. His fingers loosened, sending the phone falling. Luckily, it landed in his lap and was easily retrieved. As he pressed the receiver to his ear again, he said, "Thank you, Uncle. Seriously. You don't know how much that means to me."

Abraham paused, as if he wanted to say more, and Joss wondered briefly what that more might have been. Criticism? Further admiration? Did he dare question? "Keep up the good work, Joss. I'm headed to London in the next few weeks. I'll be sure to pass on details of your triumph to the Society elders. Have a good flight. We'll talk again soon."

"Thanks." The word escaped Joss in a near-whisper. He snapped the phone closed and, much to the flight attendant's relief, powered it down. A fog of wonder curled in around his mind. He'd left home at the beginning of the summer a divided person: Joss the boy, Joss the Slayer. But he was going home knowing who he was and where he belonged.

He was a member of the Slayer Society. And everything he did, and had done, was for the good of mankind.

And, of course, for Cecile.